T

Paris in [...] story of obsession and collaboration. When the Nazis marched into Paris a year earlier, they found an almost empty city. Hundreds of thousands of Parisians were in flight on the roads leading south. The Germans did not want an empty city. They did not want a dead Paris. Airplanes and mechanized units were immediately sent out to drive the French back to Paris. The Nazi effort succeeded, and in a few months the life of Paris was reestablished. But of course there were those who never left Paris in the first place. They saw the German occupation as an opportunity, a chance to indulge in new fancies, a chance to make a fortune, a chance to become part of the Nazi New Order. "They'll be here forever," some people said. Simone and Bernard Duchenne believed it. Simone begins a series of erotic entanglements with German officers, one colonel after the other. She becomes obsessed with the Nazis and with Adolf Hitler. In the meantime her husband Bernard has only one thought in mind: to make as much money as possible by producing SS uniforms for the German Reich. The story takes us to the streets and cafes of Paris during the occupation. Bernard's mistress is Nicole Sabatier, but unknown to Bernard, Nicole's brother Lucien is an underground saboteur who fights the Nazis. This is a dark time in the history of the French people, a time of pretense and shadows and mocking laughter. The Hour of the Wolf in Paris . . .

Other books by Blue Moon *Authors*

RICHARD MANTON

DREAM BOAT
LA VIE PARISIENNE
SWEET DREAMS
LOVE LESSONS
BELLE SAUVAGE
PEARLS OF THE ORIENT
BOMBAY BOUND

DANIEL VIAN

BLUE TANGO
SABINE
CAROUSEL
ADAGIO
BERLIN 1923

AKAHIGE NAMBAN

CHRYSANTHEMUM, ROSE, AND THE SAMURAI
SHOGUN'S AGENTS
WOMEN OF THE MOUNTAIN
WARRIORS OF THE TOWN
WOMEN OF GION

BLUE MOON BOOKS
333 Park Avenue South
New York, New York 10010

Jazz Age

THE HOUR
OF THE WOLF
PARIS 1941

DANIEL VIAN

BLUE MOON BOOKS, INC. NEW YORK

First Blue Moon Edition 1989
First Printing 1989

ISBN 0-929654-19-6

Manufactured in the United States of America
Published by Blue Moon Books, Inc.
333 Park Avenue South
New York, New York 10010

Cover design by Steven Brower

for the ghosts of Drancy

PART ONE:
OCTOBER

A gray sky. Noon. October 14.

First in view is the top of the Arc de Triomphe, only the upper third of the structure seen in the distance against a gray October sky, a flat gray western sky that shows nothing in its dull aspect. On either side of the square arch, the lines of the trees and the buildings along the Champs-Elysées radiate toward the foreground, each line of tres originating at one of the vertical pillars of the arch, the structure of the arch far enough in the distance to allow the two lines of trees to nearly converge at their origin. The trunks of the trees, the sidewalks on either side of the boulevard, are not visible. For the past few moments a murmuring sound has been heard, and now the murmur slowly grows louder as it reconstitutes itself into a series of musical sounds, musical instruments, trumpets, drums, trombones, a tuba, and finally the sound of marching feet as a steady beat under the sound of the martial music.

Still, nothing is visible yet except the upper part of

the arch in the distance and the two lines of the barren trees and the roofs of the buildings behind them, the tops of the trees and the tops of the buildings that radiate out from the arch toward the foreground.

Then slowly the view changes, pulls back, becomes more encompassing, more of the great arch in the distance, more of the trees visible, more of the buildings behind the trees, and now for the first time a figure is seen against the background of the trees on the right side. As the figure grows more distinct, it becomes evident the figure is a soldier, a man in a greyish-green uniform, a grey helmet, a high collar with a white or yellow marker of some kind on each side just below his chin. The soldier can be seen only from the middle of his chest upward, his helmet just at the level of the tops of the trees in the background. What is also evident is that the soldier's body is bobbing up and down, up and down, and after another moment it is now clear the soldier must be riding a horse, although the animal that carries him is still not visible.

The music is louder, the trumpets, the drums, the sound of the marching feet . . .

And then gradually more and more of the boulevard is revealed, the military band, the marching soldiers as they make a sharp turn to the left directly in the foreground, the soldier on the horse in the middle-ground, the arch in the distance, the military vehicles on each side of the boulevard, the scattering of pedestrians who stand right and left on the sidewalks of the boulevard as they watch the passing parade.

This is 1200 hours, and as they do every day at 1200 hours, the German soldiers of the garrison of the Kommandant von Gross-Paris are in the midst of a parade march down the Champs-Elysées.

German helmets. German soldiers. German military vehicles. And now the standard bearer of the Kommandant's garrison has approached the foreground, a soldier carrying an elaborate affair, an eagle perched on top of a circle that contains within it a tilted swastika, then below that a square of white silk and black lettering: Kommandatur Paris, and below that a large eight-pointed silver star, and below the star a silver ornament four feet wide molded in the curved shape of the horns of a huge ox, a large tassel hanging from the tip of each horn, white and black on one side, red and black on the other side, and then directly below the horns a large silver bell that is now heard to be ringing as the soldier uses his two hands to hold the entire assemblage, the pole, the bell, the horns, the tassels, the eight-pointed star, the white silk with black lettering, the tilted swastika, the brass eagle with its wings spread that rides on top of the tilted swastika as it gazes down the Champs-Elysées at 1200 hours in the month of October.

The music continues, a new squad of trumpets, the marching feet, the drums rattling again . . .

The bed is seen from above through the frame of a

skylight, the two figures sprawled across the width of the bed, the man lying partly on top of Simone as she holds her arms folded across his shoulders. The man's face is not visible. He wears nothing above the waist, grey trousers or breeches below the waist, his legs extended over the side of the bed so that his legs below the knees are not visible. As he lies partly on top of Simone, her face can be seen above his right shoulder. Her left hand rests on his neck, her right arm extended across his back. The entire length of Simone's right leg is visible, the right hip, the right thigh, the leg, the foot. She wears a white slip, either silk or cotton, but only the lower part of it can be seen and it might be only a half-slip. To the left of the two bodies sprawled on the bed are two large pillows, and then beyond the pillows the headpiece of the bed, a brass frame, vertical bars, a continuous curved bar that connects the vertical bars and completes the frame. The wall to the left is indistinct, but close to the frame of the bed the pattern of the wallpaper is suggested, broad vertical stripes, the color a dull blue against a grey background. Nothing more of the room can be seen, since everything else is obscured by the shadows, by darkness in the corners. There is no sound of any kind: the scene below the skylight is viewed in a total silence.

Then abruptly the two figures on the bed are moving, the man rolling over to lie on his right side, Simone now lying on her left side, the man's left arm across her waist, his hand on the small of her back, Simone's right arm across the man's left shoulder, her right hand at his neck. It is apparent now that Simone wears a half-slip and a brassiere, the color of the brassiere the same cream-white color as the color of the half-slip. She has her legs folded so that her right knee rests upon her left ankle. The man's legs and feet are extended, hanging over the side of the bed, and now it can be seen that he's wearing breeches and not trousers, gray breeches with a red stripe down the outer seam on each side, black boots now visible below the breeches, the boots of polished leather and shining in the light that enters from above.

The view remains as before, the bed, the two figures sprawled on the bed, everything seen from above through the skylight. And now Simone pulls away and she sits up with her weight supported by her left arm, her left leg folded under her right leg, her right ankle hanging over the edge of the bed. The man moves also, his body shifting as he rises, as he sits on the edge of the bed with his arms extended, his right hand touching Simone's left arm, his left hand holding Simone's right hand. They gaze at each other a moment. Simone moves her lips but she says nothing. Then she closes her eyes and she lowers the upper half of her body to sprawl on the bed again, across the width of the bed, the man now joining her, sprawled across the width of the bed beside her, his arms folded now and his head resting on the upper part of his folded right arm.

On the Champs-Elysées the soldiers are gone, the

parade finished, no sign of the garrison marchers. The boulevard is almost empty, a man on a bicycle on the right, a velo-taxi on the left, a motorcycle with a side-car, a military truck in the distance, several vehicles beyond that, toward the rise that obscures the lower part of the Arc de Triomphe. Scattered puddles of rainwater can be seen in the middle of the wide road. No street signs are evident. Where is it? Is it the point where the boulevard crosses the rue du Colisée? Or is it somewhere further east? On the right one can see a vertical sign over a small shop, white letters on a black background, only the lower part of the sign visible, the letters . . . OTHAIN, four people standing at the edge of the sidewalk, either preparing to cross the boulevard or just gazing at something, the man on the bicycle now passing them, the military truck now passing the velo-taxi on the left, the heavy tires rolling through one rain puddle after another as it continues toward the Place de la Concorde . . .

Simone and the man are now sprawled diagonally across the bed, the view from above as before, but now the skylight has been penetrated and the two figures and the bed are much closer, close enough so that nothing else is seen, Simone and the man extended from the lower left to the upper right. They lie on their sides facing each other, Simone on her left side, the man on his right side, the man's left arm across Simone's waist, Simone's right hand over the man's left shoulder. Their faces are almost touching. The two pillows on the left have been pushed forward so that one of the pillows is partly off the edge of the bed, the upper edge as seen in the view from above, the view from directly above the bed and above the two sprawled figures.

Simone's face: her eyes have a distant look, two eyes that seem to see nothing.

She likes the way he smells. She doesn't know why, maybe it's because he's different. Why should I like it? Why am I here? It's not real, he's a boche, isn't he? Why am I here with him? Such a little room and I thought it would be larger. Well it's not the first time is it? This is the second time with him and the first time in the other place the room was just as small as this one. What do you want? Do you know what you want? It's the uniform, isn't it? What a farce. It's a comedy on the stage. You ought to be home now, but instead here you are half naked on a bed with him. How old is he? He must be forty-five, the same age as Bernard. Or maybe he's older. You can't tell because of the coloring. Or at least I can't tell. They all look so healthy, don't they? The way they strut around in their boots. I wish he had all of his uniform on. He gets out of it so fast there's no time to look at him. You're a stupid girl, darling. You're a very stupid girl. Well, a woman anyway. I feel so lazy. I'd like to lie here all afternoon and forget about everything. Yes, why not? He's watching me, isn't he? It wasn't that bad last time and now he wants it again. I can tell by the way he looks at me that he's getting in the mood for it. Yes, he wants it all right. Anyway, it's not a trouble. I'm certainly not the one to say I mind it. Not like some. I'm not like that. I wouldn't be here if I were like that, would I? I like his smell and I like his mouth and I like his uniform even when he's wearing only part of it now. He looks healthy, doesn't he? Yes, he does look healthy, strong and healthy. They always look so strong and healthy in the uniform. The best thing is to forget about everything else and just be here.

I can't stay more than an hour, Simone says.

You're quite lovely.

Do you have other French women?

I won't say.

I don't mind.

Women always mind it.

No, really, I don't mind it. Where are you from? Did I ask you that last time?

Hamburg.

I don't know anything about Hamburg.

It doesn't matter.

On a wall in the rue Lobineau: The background of the poster is a deep red. The upper half shows only a large letter V, the letter white against the red background. Directly below the letter V is a small tilted black swastika. Below the swastika, large letters again in white: VICTORIA! And then below that three

lines of black lettering: THE TRIUMPH OF GER-
MANY WHICH FIGHTS FOR A NEW EUROPE.

Simone and the man are now sitting up on the bed.
Only the upper parts of their bodies are visible, part
of the headpiece of the bed to the right behind Simone's
back, a lampshade in the dark corner beyond the
man's head and left shoulder. His right hand is gripping the upper part of Simone's left arm. The man's
back and shoulders are bare, but Simone is still
wearing her white lace brassiere, the left cup of the
brassiere showing the fine lacework stretched by the
fullness of her left breast. Their faces are close together and Simone has her eyes lowered, her head
tilted slightly toward her left shoulder as if she waits
for him. Yes, she does wait. He leans forward now
and he presses his lips against hers. He continues to
grip her left arm as he kisses her mouth. Simone's
eyes remain closed as he kisses her. Then finally he
pulls back. He kisses her once again and then once
again he pulls back.

I envy your husband, the man says.

Please don't talk about my husband.

Yes, of course.

Now his right hand moves, his hand releasing its
grip on the upper part of her left arm and his fingers
pulling back, sliding across the arm to touch the
lacework of the left cup of Simone's brassiere. His
fingertips graze over the covered globe of her breast,

over the upper surface, around the outside curve, across the underslope. The palm of his hand never touches her breast. And now his head moves forward and they kiss. Simone's face is tilted as he presses his lips against hers. Then his hands are moving again, both hands sliding around her back to touch the hooks that hold her brassiere in place. They continue kissing as he unhooks the brassiere, as he pulls the shoulder-straps down, as he draws the cups away from her breasts while his lips are pressed against hers. —

Then his face pulls away, his lips pulling free of her lips, his head tilting down as he gazes at her exposed breasts.

What does he think? What does he think when he looks at me? It's my body, isn't it? What does he think now?

Simone's breasts have light brown nipples. The two globes are firm enough to stand out aggressively from her chest. She watches the man's face as he looks at her.

Did you suckle your child?

Yes, Simone says.

He slides his hand under her left breast and he lifts the breast as he kisses her mouth again.

On a wall in the rue Colbert, a posted notice, red lettering and a black border: 1. The Jew TYSZELMAN Szmul of Paris, 2. The man called GAUTHEROT

Henry of Paris, have been condemned to death for
HELPING THE ENEMY, having taken part in a
communist demonstration directed against the troops
of the German occupation. THEY HAVE BEEN
SHOT TODAY, Paris, 19 August 1941, THE MILI-
TARY TRIBUNAL.

Simone and the man are naked on the bed, Simone
on her back seen from her left side, her knees pulled
backward until they almost touch her shoulders, her
thighs parallel with her body, her legs bent at the
knees and vertical, her legs and thighs forming a
right angle between them, the soles of her feet pointing at the ceiling over the bed.

The man is on all fours crouched over Simone's
body so that her legs lie along his shoulders, her left
leg along his right arm and shoulder, her right leg
along his left arm and shoulder. Since Simone is seen
from her left side, not everything on her right side is
visible. The man supports the weight of the front part
of his body with his hands, his right hand adjacent to
Simone's left shoulder and his left hand presumably
adjacent to Simone's right shoulder. The weight of
the rear part of his body is supported by his knees,
each knee adjacent to one of Simone's hips, his right
knee touching her left hip, his left knee presumably
touching her right hip as she continues to hold her
knees pulled back to her shoulders.

The position of the two bodies is such that it's not

apparent whether or not the man is actually penetrating Simone's sex with his member.

The bed has a dark blue counterpane. Nothing is visible on the wall beyond the far side of the bed except part of a curtain at the extreme left that apparently covers a small window.

The man moves. He pulls his body back and he sits on his heels. Simone now straightens her legs, pushes them forward so that her calves now rest against his shoulders, her torso and head horizontal, her legs vertical, the soles of her bare feet still pointing at the ceiling.

It's crazy, isn't it, the way he has me? I shouldn't be here. A woman with a husband shouldn't be here. Not here. In a moment my legs will hurt, and then my back. Dear God, the way he looks at me.

The man extends his arms forward and he closes his hands over Simone's breasts.

You're very French, the man says. Have you always lived in Paris?

Yes.

And your husband?

No, he's from Lyon.

What kind of business does he make?

He owns a cloth factory.

Cloth?

Military blankets now. For the Germans.

I see.

Please . . .

What?

Please don't talk about my husband.

* * *

On a wall in the rue Quinault, a posted notice: Prefecture of Police. ONE MILLION REWARD. Notice to the population. Recently, several offenses have been committed against the tracks and property of the railroad. These offenses place in danger human lives and especially the thousands of workers who each day use this means of transportation. These offenses interrupt communications and compromise the handling of the already difficult current situation. As a consequence, the entire population, in the general interest, is invited to associate itself with the repression and prevention of these offenses. A REWARD OF ONE MILLION FRANCS IS OFFERED TO ANY PERSON WHO MAKES POSSIBLE THE ARREST OF THE PERPETRATORS OF COMMITTED OFFENSES. The most absolute discretion is assured. There are means available for furnishing useful information to the Prefecture of Police. Order of the Police Judiciary—56, Quai des Orfèvres. Telephone: Turbigo 92-00. P.O. Box 557.

Simone's legs are down. She lies with her head turned to the side, toward her left shoulder. Her eyes are closed and her thighs are spread wide apart. The man has now dropped the lower part of his body, the weight of the upper part of his body supported by his arms, one arm on each side of Simone as he pushes himself between her open thighs, as he pushes his penis inside her sex, moves his hips, pulls back a bit and then pushes forward again. Simone's hands are at the joining of her thighs. She keeps her eyes closed as her fingers press on either side of her penetrated sex. The man's head is bent as he gazes at their joining. Now he lifts his head and he looks at Simone's face.

Am I hurting you?

Simone opens her eyes. She turns her head and she looks at him: No.

Is it good for you?

Yes.

He moves again. He leans forward to rest the upper part of his body against Simone, his chest against her breasts, the right side of his face against the left side of Simone's face, his hands reaching back to hold Simone's buttocks as he continues moving his hips, pushing and pulling back, pushing and pulling back.

Simone lifts her legs and she raises her knees. She crosses her ankles over his buttocks and she groans as his penis continues to move inside her.

On a wall in the Avenue de Messine: NOTICE. On 21 August in the morning, a member of the German army was the victim of an assassination in Paris. As a consequence I order the following: 1. Beginning 23 August all French persons already under arrest by the German authorities in France, or who will be arrested by the same authorities in the future, will be considered as hostages. 2. In case of a new offense, a number of hostages corresponding to the gravity of the offense will be shot. Paris, 22 August 1941. For the Militarbefehlschaber in Frankreich SCHAUMBURG Generalleutnant.

The man is now standing and he wears the gray breeches that show a red stripe on each side. His chest is bare. Simone still lies on the bed, her body now covered by a sheet.

The man's face: his head is turned as he looks at Simone. His face is empty.

He puts on a grey shirt. Simone watches him. Then he sits on the edge of the bed and he pulls onto his legs a pair of black leather boots. He rises and he stomps his feet one after the other to get them firmly in place. Then he pulls a dark green tunic off the back of a chair and he slips it on, over his arms and shoulders, standing erect now as he buttons the tunic front. When he completes the closing of the tunic, he reaches for the black leather belt that lies dangling over the back of the nearby chair. He circles his waist with the belt, tightens the belt and buckles it. The pistol holster attached to the belt on his left side is now visible.

You look very official, Simone says. Will you be a general someday?

The man stares at Simone: Yes, why not? I should be a colonel in six months, and after that there are possibilities.

Simone looks at the window, and then she looks at the man again.

His face shows a thin smile as he tugs at the tunic of his uniform.

Kiss me again, she says.

He comes toward her. He leans over her as she half-reclines on the bed. She touches his arm with her hand, her fingertips sliding over the braid on his cuff and then over his chest to touch one of the silver buttons. When she lifts her face, he kisses her mouth.

Simone's hand: the fingers are now clutching at the sleeve of his tunic.

Oh yes, yes oh yes, am I coming again? I'm coming, oh yes I'm coming again, oh God yes . . .

Two women walk arm in arm on the Pont Neuf.

We'll have a cold winter, one woman says.

Don't say that, the other woman says.

Well, it's better to know the truth, isn't it?

A clicking of heels in the Avenue Marceau, a German sergeant laughing at something. And now suddenly Simone appears as she turns the corner into the avenue. The major's name is Hans Quiring. I'll never call him Hans. I like the Quiring better. It's odd, isn't it? And he's so correct, my boche. You have a boche, don't you? He lives with that pack of officers in the Majestic. Administrative duties, he says: the occupation of a city like Paris can be quite complicated. Well, never mind that. I don't want to think about that.

Two velo-taxis pass each other in the empty road, each driver puffing as he pedals his vehicle.

She gazes at the shop windows as she walks past them. My blond boche. Is it true the peasants in Normandy are descended from the Danes? It's an adventure, isn't it? It's quite an adventure, darling. Oh yes it is. You can't deny the excitement. Bernard would be furious of course. She imagines Bernard's eyes in the midst of one of his rages. Then she thinks of the major again, the bed in the hotel room, his hands, his thrusting. And his uniform. She wanted him to take her while he was wearing his uniform, but she was too modest to suggest it. A shudder passes through her as she remembers the way his hands stroked her breasts.

Now a military motorcyclist dressed in black leather zooms down the avenue, passes Simone and vanishes behind her.

The conquerors. The major is one of the conquerors. Bernard likes to think we're simply being absorbed into something more important, but it's still a conquest, isn't it? A conquest with a smell of leather. You're a collabo, darling. You're sleeping with a boche. But what a pleasure. Is it the infidelity? Whatever it is, the excitement is enough to make her quiver whenever she thinks of it. You're quivering now, aren't you, darling?

A flock of birds appears from the east, the flock

circling over the avenue before heading west toward
the Bois.

Bernard is not to know. He never knows, does he?
He's not to know about my boche. She thinks of the
bed again, her body under his body, her thighs gripping his waist, then afterward the uniform, the kiss,
did I really come when he kissed me? Did I really
come? Yes I did yes I did . . .

Now suddenly two black uniforms appear at the
next corner, two officers in the SS, black peaked
caps, black boots, an armband showing a swastika on
each left arm. Simone quivers as she gazes at them,
as she walks toward them. She trembles as she watches
them cross the road. Then she forces her eyes to turn
away. She finds a shop window and she stares at the
reflection of her own face.

On the door of the Hotel Drouot: Communiqué
from the Prefecture of Police. On the order of the
Commissariat General of Jewish questions, the entrance of JEWS into the auction rooms of the hotel is
ABSOLUTELY FORBIDDEN.

Bernard stands in a room with a young woman
named Nicole. Part of a bed can be seen on the left
beyond Nicole's back, a lampshade in the right beyond
Bernard's shoulder, the far wall, a small painting on
the right side of the wall, a picture of a house and

possibly a street. The view of most of the painting is
blocked by Nicole's head. They stand close to each
other, in each other's arms, facing each other so that
Bernard is seen in left profile and Nicole in right
profile. They are both dressed. Nicole wears a white
blouse. Bernard wears a white shirt and a blue tie.
Bernard's left hand is on Nicole's back just under her
right shoulder. Nicole's right arm is raised, her right
hand lying flat against Bernard's left cheek. Bernard
bends his head a bit as he gazes at Nicole's uptilted
face. Is Nicole smiling? Barnard's back is illumi-
nated by sunlight and one supposes the shutters of an
unseen window have been opened on the right side.

Do you like it? Bernard says.

Yes, I like it, Nicole says.

How soon will you move in?

I don't know. Tomorrow, I think.

Yes, tomorrow. I want you to move in tomorrow.
I want you to be here tomorrow.

All right.

On a wall in the rue Ernestine: DECREE! Listening to foreign radio stations and the diffusion of news
from foreign radio stations is prohibited. Violators
will be severely punished in accordance with the
decree introducing the German penal code of 10 May
1940. Listening to the following radio stations from
German transmitter posts is permitted: Stations in the
Protectorate of Bohemia and Moravia, Holland, Bel-
gium, Luxembourg, from the occupied zones of Nor-

way, Poland, France, and also from radio stations of Lyon, Marseilles, and Toulouse. The Chief of Military Administration in France. 14 August 1940—Montrichard—imp. Pinguet.

Only Nicole is visible. The buttons of her blouse have been undone in the front, the blouse pulled to each side so that the inner slopes of her breasts are revealed. The bed can be seen behind her, but most of it is in shadows. Nicole's hair has fallen forward on her left side so that her left eye is partly hidden. She looks directly at the viewer. Her right arm moves, but her right hand cannot be seen. Her face is without expression.

On a wall in the rue Rampal: NOTICE. 1) Roger-Henry NOGARÈDE of Paris, 2) Alfred OTTINO of Saint-Ouen, 3) Andre SIGONNEY of Drancy, 4) Raymond JUSTICE of Drancy, 5) Jean-Louis RAPINAT of Pavillons-sous-Bois have been condemned to death by court-martial for helping the enemy, having taken part in a communist demonstration directed against the German army. They have been shot. Paris, 27 August 1941. Der Militarbefehlshaber in Frankreich.

Bernard and Nicole. His shirt has been opened and peeled back to expose his chest and shoulders and the upper part of his right arm. The lower part of Nicole's body is not visible, but she appears to be kneeling in front of him and the implication is that she's naked. She has both arms raised, her hands pushing Bernard's undershirt upward to expose his chest and belly. He still wears his trousers. Nicole has her face pressed against Bernard's body at the level of his navel. Bernard's head is bent as he gazes down at her. Nicole kisses his belly. Bernard mumbles something, the words hardly audible. The wall behind them is in shadows, but part of a curtain can be seen on the right.

Nicole drops her hands now, and Bernard's undershirt falls down to cover his chest. Her fingers work at the buttons of his trousers, undoing the buttons, pulling at his trousers, pulling at his drawers.

Bernard's face: he bends his head, his eyes almost closed as he watches Nicole.

Now his trousers and drawers are down at his thighs and Nicole has his genitals in her hands. She holds his testicles with her left hand and his penis with her right hand. She extends her tongue and she slowly licks the glans of his penis.

On a wall in the rue Camou: NOTICE. 1. Marine lieutenant Henri Louis Honoré COMTE D'ESTIENNES D'ORVES, French, born 5 June 1901 in Verrières, 2. the commercial agent Maurice Charles Emile BARLIER, French, born 9 September 1905 in St.

-Dié, 3. the merchant Jan Louis-Guilleaume DOORNIK, Dutch, born 26 June 1905 in Paris, have been condemned to death for sabotage. They were shot today. Paris, 29 August 1941. Der Militarbefehlshaber in Frankreich.

Nicole lies on the bed on her back, her legs raised, her thighs open. Bernard is extended between Nicole's thighs, his penis moving inside her sex. Nicole's left hand rests on her left thigh, her fingers almost touching her left buttock, the hand and wrist visible under Bernard's right forearm. Her left leg is folded at the knee in the crook of Bernard's left elbow. On the other side of Bernard, Nicole's right leg is visible only from the knee down to the foot, her right thigh completely hidden by Bernard's body. Nicole lies with her head back, her head resting on a small salmon-colored pillow, her eyes closed. Bernard's face is flushed. He continues moving his hips, his penis slowly moving in and out of Nicole's sex. The pink bag of his testicles is visible as it moves with his penis. One can see the stretching of the hairy lips of Nicole's sex, the penis sliding back, pushing forward again, the quivering of the flesh of Nicole's left buttock.

On a wall in the rue de Sully: NOTICE. On 6, 10, and 11 September 1941, certain hostilities were committed in Paris against some members of the German army. As a measure of repression against these cowardly offenses, the following hostages were shot in accordance with my ordinance of 22 August 1941: 1.) MATHERON, Lucien, René. Born 8 October 1920. 2.) JOLY, René, Louis. Born 12 January 1900. 3.) CLEMENT, Lucien, Léon. Born 24 June 1912. 4.) GOKELAERE, Albert, Valentin. Born 1 April 1915. 5.) BONNIN, André. Born 12 May 1917. 6.) LIBERMANN, David. Born 1 February 1922. 7.) MAGER-OPAL, Chil. Born 20 August 1891. 8.) BERNHEIM, Isador. Born 1 February 1869. 9.) BECKERMANN, Henri. Born 12 July 1920. 10.) BLUM, Lucien. Born 2 August 1879. Paris 16 September 1941. Der Militarbefehlshaber in Frankreich von STULPNAGEL General der Infanterie.

Bernard is standing now. Nicole kneels on the bed in front of him. Nicole's buttocks and sex are completely revealed, the anus, the hair in the split between the globes of the buttocks, the hairy pouch of the bulging sex at the joining of her thighs. Bernard's hands are placed on the upper slopes of Nicole's buttocks, his left hand on her left buttock, his right hand on her right buttock. Bernard's penis fills the mouth of Nicole's sex, his member slowly sliding in and out of the stretched opening. His testicles jiggle as he pushes forward. Nicole's head is turned so that the upper part of her face is visible beyond her left shoulder. The small globe of her left breast hangs down, the nipple almost touching the yellow counterpane that covers the bed. Beyond Nicole's head is a blank wall, streaked beige wallpaper, the corner at the far right in shadows.

You're a sweet girl, Bernard says.

It feels good, Nicole says.

You like it, don't you?

Yes, I like it.

Bernard chuckles. He pinches her right buttock with his fingers and he pushes his penis forward again

On a wall in the Avenue Kléber: NOTICE. On 16 September 1941, a cowardly assassination was again committed on the person of a German soldier. As a measure of repression against this crime, the following hostages have been shot: 1. PITARD, George, of Paris. Civil servant, communist. 2. HAJJE, Antoine, of Paris. Civil servant, communist. 3. ROLNIKAS, Michelis, (Jew), of Paris. Propagator of communist ideas. 4. NAIN, Adrien, of Paris. Author of communist tracts. 5. PEYRAT, Roger, of Paris. Aggression against German soldiers. 6. MARCHAL, Victor, of Paris. Aggression against German soldiers. 7. ANJO-LVY, René, Lucien, of Paris-Gentilly. Distributor of communist tracts. 8. HERPIN, François, of Paris-Malakoff. Communist cell chief, sabotage. 9. GUIG-NOIS, Pierre, of Ivry-sur-Seine. Possession of communist tracts, possession of arms. 10. MASSET, Georges, of Paris. Possession of illegal arms. 11. LOUBIER, Daniel, of Paris. Possession of illegal arms. 12. PEUREUX, Maurice, of Paris-Montreuil. Possession of illegal arms. I draw attention to the fact that in case of a recurrence a more considerable number of hostages will be shot. Der Militarbefehlshaber in Frankreich von STULPNAGEL General der Infanterie. Paris, 20 September 1941.

Bernard is now standing in the Sèvres metro station. He keeps his back stiff. He gazes at the others who wait on the platform for the next train. Thank God he wasn't stupid enough to abandon Paris. To go where? Marseilles? The hell with that. He couldn't live in Marseilles. And in any case the future is here and not there. Here in Paris. He turns to look at a quartet of German soldiers, young boys in their greyish-green uniforms, two of them with machine-pistols. The Fritz. He doesn't care one way or the other. Better than the idiots they had before, the Blum crowd. He knew a long time ago it would lead to no good. Let the goats build shelters in the Vosges. Nicole is certainly a delight now, completely absorbed in doing nothing, she says, so thankful for the little flat. Always keep them thankful, sir. The way she kneels on the bed to turn up that pink bottom. As hairy as a bear down there. Oh yes. Well, you like it, don't you? Between the legs she's ten years older.

What an absurdity. Not at all like Simone. Madame
remains a lady in any position. Simone is a woman to
have on his arm and Nicole is a girl to have kneeling
on a bed. Nicole accepts everything, Simone accepts
nothing. So you have it for Nicole, do you? Yes, you
do, don't you? But with ease, you fool. Don't become entangled again. It's never good to be entangled.
Progress occurs only with compromise. Yes, that's
the motto. Progress occurs only with compromise.
You know what you want, don't you? It's always
important to know what you want. A man has to be
aware of the opportunities in his life, the important
moments, the important opportunities. All these idiots who go crazy buying gold. No, that's not the
way. What's needed now is a bit of cleverness, a
proper connection, the right sort of contract, show
them you can be useful. There's enough for everyone,
isn't there? They need good people here, they do
need good people, they always need good people . . .

In a shoe store in the rue de Provence. The shopgirl stands with two German soldiers, two privates in
forage caps. The girl stands on the left with an open
shoe box in her hands. She wears a black dress
buttoned to the neck, her face seen in profile from her
right side. In the center is the taller of the two
soldiers, his right arm raised and folded and the
fingers of his right hand (except the thumb) slipped

into the opening of his tunic. The other soldier holds a black boot in his left hand, his right hand raised so that his fingers touch his neck on the right side. The soldier who holds the boot gazes at it. The other soldier smiles at him, and then he turns to smile at the shopgirl. He says something in German. The shopgirl blushes and shakes her head.

Simone appears, seen only from above the waist. She wears a tailored jacket over a dark blue blouse. Behind her is one of the windows of the Duchenne flat, part of a drape on the right side. The window appears to look out on a courtyard, but the view beyond Simone is too blurred to distinguish details. She stands facing the viewer, her head turned slightly toward her left shoulder as she gazes at something or someone out of view on the right.

Now Bernard can be seen seated at the dining room table. The view is from the level of the table on the opposite side and facing Bernard. He holds something in his right hand, maybe a piece of bread. On the left, part of the large fireplace is visible. Behind Bernard is a curtained window. Directly in front of him, and partly blocking the view, is a large soup tureen. A small figurine can be seen on the mantle over the fireplace, but the mantle is partly in shadow and the subject of the figurine is obscure.

Now Simone again. She appears to have moved away from the window, and now she stands to the

right of Bernard at the edge of the round table.
Behind Simone is an open door to another room, a
curtained window at the far end of that room. More
of the dining room table is visible now. Bernard has
a flat dinner plate in front of him, maybe a dish of
meat and vegetables, two knives on the left side of
the plate, a large bowl of vegetables or potatoes on
the other side of the plate. Bernard is now sitting
back with his arms folded as he looks at Simone. She
stands there to his right with a knife and fork in her
hands, the fork in her left hand, the knife in her right
hand, a dark mass of meat on a plate in front of her
hands. The hands are positioned as if she's about to
cut the meat, but at the moment her head is turned
toward her left as she looks at Bernard. On the wall
at the right beyond Bernard, the bottom of a large
framed picture can be seen, and below that a round
framed photograph of a woman, the sort of photograph commonly made during the years of the twenties.

How much do you want? Simone says.

No more, Bernard says. I'm not hungry.

Are you sure?

Yes, of course I'm sure. I've had enough.

It's really shameful to waste it. It's nearly a whole
ration ticket.

Don't be stupid, we can get all we want from
Labiche. I told you that. All the meat we want.

One day they'll catch Labiche and hang him.

Don't be silly, not Labiche. He's one of their
customers. He buys everything from the Gestapo.

Oh God. Are you sure you won't eat any more?

I can't eat if I'm not hungry.

I'll have to give it to the cook.

All right, give it to the cook then. I don't care.

What's the matter with you?

My God, nothing is the matter with me, I'm just not hungry.

Simone puts down the knife and fork. She stands there a moment holding her hands as she gazes down at the plate of beef.

Simone's hands: her left hand is closed over her right hand, her left thumb along her right wrist, the fingers of her left hand curled under her right palm.

Now the hands move. She drops her right hand and she picks up the knife again. She takes the fork in her left hand and she begins cutting at the meat. She cuts two slices, places the slices on a plate, and then she puts the knife and fork down on the table beside the meat tray.

The view changes, and now Simone is completely visible as she carries the plate to the side of the table opposite Bernard. She sits down in the empty chair and she begins eating.

What did you do today? Bernard says.

Nothing, Simone says with a shrug. I went shopping. The stores are empty as usual. All the good things are gone. Shipped to Germany, I suppose. Everything is gone.

Not everything.

Almost everything.

All right, almost everything. Well, what do you expect? They're fighting a war, aren't they?

I don't want to argue, Simone says.

It's just talk. The bastards are here and what's in the shops doesn't mean a damn thing one way or the other. So far we're not doing too badly at all. Don't you agree? You have everything you want, don't you?

Yes.

I told you. I told you with money it doesn't matter. As long as the money comes in, it doesn't matter. I'm working to get a big contract. Something new.

Something new?

Uniforms. They need uniforms, don't they? I can easily convert the machines to making the cloth for uniforms. Then I put together a shop to cut and stitch and press and we give them a finished uniform. I'm talking about something big, a big contract, a big company. Much better than a contract for blankets.

Uniforms for the army?

Yes, uniforms for the army. For the Wermacht, for the SS, for the Gestapo, whatever they want. That's millions of uniforms, isn't it?

Yes.

It's business. Now the old life is finished.

In all the colors? Simone says.

What colors?

The uniforms. They have different colors.

Black, green, brown, it doesn't make any difference. They can have any color they want.

Maybe they won't choose you for the contract.

Don't worry about that. I'm getting to know the right people.

You won't forget about tomorrow night, will you?
What's happening tomorrow night?
We have tickets for the opera.
Good. That's good. That's a good way to relax.

Later Simone is in another room, a child's room.
The girl lies in her bed as she smiles at Simone.
Hello, Mommy.
Hello, darling.
Simone feels the wine she had at dinner. Her
cheeks are flushed. She sits down on the edge of the
bed and she strokes Marie-Claire's face. A wave of
tenderness passes through Simone as she gazes at her
daughter. The girl is a wonder, a child, a person, six
years old, an object of Simone's love.
I want to love her, Simone thinks, I do love her,
yes I do love her.
Goodnight, darling.
Simone kisses Marie-Claire. The child smiles and
closes her eyes.

Mid-afternoon inside the Cafe Le Colisée on the
Champs-Elysées, the brown tables, the red chairs,
the ornate chandeliers. A woman with a black jacket,
a red purse, a red plaid skirt and black shoes appears
in the foreground, her face turned away from the
viewer as she gazes at the crowd, her left foot lifted,
the toe pointed at the floor as she continues to walk

by. In a moment two German officers, one with a short dark moustache, follow the same path between the tables, across the foreground from right to left, the officer on the right holding something in his hands, a magazine or a newspaper, the officer on the left (the one with the moustache) swinging his arms in a brisk military manner, his head turned to glance at the tables, at the people, civilians, women wearing large hats, a sprinkling of Germans in uniform, two waiters in white jackets and dark trousers.

Simone sits alone at a table in the rear. She wears a black coat with a large fur collar, a red hat with a sprig of green on the crown, the hat tilted forward so that her eyes are almost hidden by the soft brim. A cup of tea and a small teapot sit on the table in front of her. She looks at the crowd, her eyes returning again and again to the entrance of the cafe, the distant pedestrians on the sidewalk seen through the enormous windows. And then finally she sees him, the major entering the door, surveying the tables, locating Simone at their usual place of rendezvous. He stands erect, the peak of his officer's cap making him appear so much taller than the others around him.

And so conspicuous, Simone thinks. I must be crazy. But this is where they usually meet and so far she's never seen anyone at all that she knows, not here, not in the Le Colisée which is now the gathering place for black marketeers and young people who drink too much. But it's dangerous, isn't it? There might be a friend of Bernard's in the crowd. What would she say? What would she tell Bernard? He's an officer I met at the German Institute. Well yes, why not that? He asked me to have tea with him and I was afraid to refuse. He knows my name. In any case he was very correct and so on. And of course Hans laughs and he says half the people here are crooks and the other half work for the Gestapo, so what difference does it make? We have to meet somewhere and this crowd is big enough to hide us, isn't it?

Quiring has now sat down at Simone's table. He smiles at her. He orders a pot of tea and he smiles at her again. My lover, Simone thinks. My lover in his lovely uniform. Those lovely epaulettes. Today he wears a leather strap diagonally across his chest from his right shoulder to his left hip.

I found a flat for us, Quiring says.

A flat?

In the rue Lavoisier. There's no need for us to meet here any more. Aren't you happy now?

Yes, I'm happy, Simone thinks. Are they looking at me? The eyes of the others? Bernard is right, we're in the middle of things. But you want it, don't you, darling? You want it and you're trembling with anticipation, aren't you? It's the uniform, isn't it? You can't look at it without trembling like a school-girl. A flat in the rue Lavoisier, a flat for the two of us, a meeting place. It's almost domestic. That's amusing, isn't it? It's almost domestic . . .

This is the rue Delambre, the sidewalk here now filled with a line of people in front of a small bakery.

On the left are two members of the French police
assigned to keep order. One of the gendarmes has his
back to the viewer. The other gendarme stands beside
the shop doorway from whence the line originates, or
to which the line is moving. A man wearing a suit
and no tie and carrying a package has apparently just
emerged from the shop, and now he walks behind the
two gendarmes and he hurries away to the left. The
people in the line are mostly women, one of them on
the extreme right with a small girl who holds the bar
of a perambulator that might contain another child.
Now one of the gendarmes turns to the line and he
raises his right arm as he calls out to the crowd: NO
MORE. NO MORE BREAD!

In the flat in the rue Lavoisier, Simone is seen
holding onto the edge of a wall with her left hand. She
wears a white blouse and a dark skirt. Behind her is a
doorway to what might be a small dressing room. As
she holds onto the edge of the wall with her left
hand, she bends to the right side, her right hand on
the heel of her right shoe, now pulling the shoe off
her foot, dropping the shoe to the floor and then
straightening her body again. Quiring has just ap-
peared in the doorway to the right, leaning forward
as he gazes at Simone, at the way she stands now in
her stocking feet on the carpet.

Do you like it? Quiring says.

Yes, Simone says.

She does like it. Five large rooms, decent furniture. Where are the people? What happened to them? Paintings and photographs on the walls, an old woman, an old man with a beard. Don't ask, darling. There's an occupation, you know. We have the boches in Paris this year. Bernard is right when he says never ask too many questions. This is a new time and it doesn't do any good to pretend it doesn't exist. It's not clever, is it? They won't be gone next week. And I don't want him to be gone anyway. They'll be here for years and years and maybe forever and ever, and as long as they don't make everyone speak German what difference does it make? What difference does it make anyway? At least to us. In a few minutes I'm going to be naked with him and then it's just the two of us.

In each other's arms now, Simone and Quiring standing against the white wall, his left arm around her right shoulder, his left hand at the back of her head, Simone's face tilted upward, the fingers of her left hand visible on his right shoulder, their faces almost touching, their lips almost touching.

They turn, a full turn so that now it's Simone who is against the wall, Quiring's mouth now pressed against hers, the fingers of her right hand now visible below his neck, below the collar of his uniform. His right arm lifts, his right hand sliding over her hair, Simone's left arm lifting to drape over his right shoulder.

I thought about you all morning, Quiring says.

Simone says nothing. Their bodies are not visible below their shoulders, but the implication is that he presses against her, presses her into the white wall.

Yes, I like the smell of him, Simone thinks. I don't know why. I do like the smell. It's like leather today, leather and tobacco, and his body is so hard, not like Bernard, no belly at all, nothing down there except the pushing of his affair. I can feel it pushing, the way he pushes his tongue at me. I can taste it. What does he think? What does he think of me? Does he ever think of his wife? Hamburg he says. I don't know about Hamburg. I don't know anything about Hamburg.

She feels the buttons, the buttons of his uniform, the braid, the leather of his belt, the heavy cloth of his tunic . . .

And now the view has suddenly changed and Simone and Quiring are seen standing near a window, a wall on the left, part of the window on the right, the long curtains, the panes of clear glass, beyond the window a suggestion of another building, other windows, other rooms. He has his tunic and shirt removed. He wears only his white undershirt and grey trousers. His right arm is around Simone's waist, holding her pressed against him as his left hand lifts her right leg, as his fingers curl behind her knee to lift her leg. Simone's dress has been raised to uncover her buttocks. Her briefs are gone, her buttocks naked. Her dress is gathered at her waist, below the gathering the edge of a white suspender belt, and then below that her buttocks, her white thighs, the dark tops of her brown stockings, her black shoes with high heels, the right shoe in the air as Quiring continues to hold her leg with his hand. Simone's face is lifted as Quiring presses his mouth against her chin.

Whose flat is this? Simone says.

Jews, Quiring says. Communists.

How many?

He laughs: Who knows? I don't know anything about them. I had a friend obtain the keys for me.

Then another view and Quiring is now sitting on a chair or on the edge of a bed while Simone stands in front of him with her arms over his shoulders and her head bent so that her lips touch his forehead. Her dress is still gathered at her waist, and as Quiring's arms encircle the lower part of her body, his right hand lies extended on the small of her back, his left forearm below her buttocks, his left hand closed over her left buttock, his thumb in the crack between the two buttocks, his fingers gripping the globe, squeezing it, the hand shifting downward to move over the tops of her stockings, shifting upward to close over the left buttock again . . .

In the Magasins du Printemps department store:

two German girls in uniform, auxiliary helpers known to the Germans as Blitzmädchen, stand in front of a display table covered with an assortment of blouses in various colors. One of the girls is standing with her hands clasped at her waist and her eyes on something beyond the table. The other girl has her hands in the pile of clothes. This girl is blonde and her military forage cap is tilted to the right side so that nearly all of her head on the left side is visible. One can see the blonde hair is carefully pinned at the side and at the nape of her neck. On the upper part of the left sleeve of her uniform is an insignia, a jagged line that ends in an arrow pointing downward. She holds a black leather portfolio or purse under her left arm, as does the other girl. Now the blonde girl tosses a blouse away and she turns to her friend and says: Let's go.

Only part of Quiring's body can be seen. He is evidently standing, while Simone appears to be kneeling in front of him. Both Simone and Quiring show no evidence of any clothing. Part of his left forearm and his left hand are seen, the hand holding the back of her head. She has her mouth closed over the front end of his penis, her lips pushed forward and relaxed, her eyes closed, her body turned slightly so that her left breast touches his left thigh. Quiring continues to hold her head with his hand as her mouth slowly moves back and forth along the length of his organ.

Wait, Quiring says. I want to sit down.

Simone pulls her mouth off the end of his penis. She looks up at him and she says nothing.

Well, he's not Bernard, she thinks. He's not Bernard, is he? He's not Bernard and he does as he pleases. I don't mind it. I like it. Yes, you do like it, don't you? Even without his lovely uniform. His pipe in my mouth, the warm blood, the wet sucking. It's all the same everywhere, isn't it? The boches are no different. The asparagus beneath the uniform, the asparagus in the breeches. Well, you knew that, didn't you? Pink and hot. He knows I like it. He knows more than Bernard, doesn't he? Yes, he does know more than Bernard . . .

Quiring is now seated in an armchair. His thighs are wide apart, his genitals exposed, his erect penis, the bloated sac that holds his testicles, the blonde hair on his belly and around his genitals and on the insides of his thighs.

Simone is kneeling on the carpet in front of Quiring and once again she has his penis in her mouth. Her lips cover only the glans. Her face is seen from the left side and her eyes appear to be closed. Her body is not visible below the upper part of her breasts. Quiring's arms are extended forward, both hands grasping Simone's head, his fingers tangled in her hair as he gazes down at her face.

Now she moves. Her mouth pushes forward, her lips sliding down to engulf more and more of the pink member that rises almost vertically from the sac of the testicles below it. When her mouth has covered three-quarters of the length of the penis, she stops moving, hesitates and begins to pull back. But Quiring prevents it. He pushes at her head now, pushes down, forces her mouth to take more of his penis. The stretching of Simone's lips is evident, the flush in her cheeks, her wet lips as they slide further and further down to the base of the pink organ.

Abruptly she pulls back, her head twisting as she finally frees herself and releases his penis from her dripping mouth.

No, Simone says. It's not possible.

Quiring keeps his thighs wide apart: You said you wanted it.

Yes, I did. But it's too much.

Pity.

I suppose the whores do it better.

The girls in Paris are quite talented.

Simone flushes: I don't care.

Quiring smiles, his right hand touching her chin: Don't be angry. You look more beautiful when you're not angry.

But I'm not angry. I'm really not angry.

In the rue de Rivoli, a stretch of the colonnade,

pedestrians strolling over the small square tiles of the walkway. Two swastikas are visible. One is in the background, at the end of the colonnade, a tilted swastika on a flag that hangs from the top of the arch over the walkway, over the heads of the pedestrians that pass beneath it. The other swastika is in the middle-ground, at the left end of a long sign over the front of a bookshop. This swastika, which is also tilted, is located within a serrated circle that resembles the outline of a machine gear. The sign itself reads: FRONTBUCHHANDLUNG. A German officer is seen in the left foreground with his back turned to the viewer as he peers into the adjacent shop window. A woman who is walking past him has just turned her head to look at the same window. The other pedestrians in the foreground have their backs to the viewer as they proceed along the walkway toward the flag in the distance.

Quiring has slumped forward, pushed his pelvis forward as Simone straddles him. He holds her buttocks with his hands. Her knees are on the seat of the armchair on either side of his hips, each hand grasping at one of the arms of the chair as she supports her weight. Her head is lifted and turned toward her right shoulder, her right breast pushed into Quiring's forehead. His penis can be seen stretching the mouth of her sex. Simone pushes down. She moans. She pulls up again. Behind them is a curtained window, on the left side the leaves and branches of a large rubber plant. Quiring's eyes are closed. Simone's eyes are closed. She pushes down again. She moans.

In the Louvre: thirteen German soldiers wearing forage caps are seen grouped around a sculpture of a reclining figure on a bed, the entire sculpture supported by a block of marble approximately three feet high. The soldiers stand right and left and at the rear, so that the sign describing the sculpture is visible in the foreground. The sign is a rectangle framed in brass, the white card containing four lines. Only the first line is legible: HERMAPHRODITE ENDORMI. The figure of the sculpture lies on a bed, the dorsal aspect uppermost, the buttocks prominent. Three of the soldiers in the background are looking directly down at the reclining figure. One of these soldiers appears to have just said something and some of the others in the group are either smiling or laughing in response to his remark.

On the bed now. Simone lies on her back, her buttocks near the edge of the bed, Quiring's hands grasping her ankles as he pushes her legs back toward her face. Once again his penis is in her sex, only the glans now, the entire length of his member visible, his scrotum a large hairy pouch at the joining of his thighs. Simone's mouth is open, her eyes closed, each hand supporting a knee as Quiring continues to push her legs back. His pelvis jerks forward, pulls back, jerks forward again. He gazes at Simone's face as his organ continues moving in her sex.

The angle of view changes and abruptly Simone's buttocks are seen at close range. Her face is visible at the upper left. Her eyes are open now. Nothing can be seen of Quiring except a part of each thigh, his swollen testicles, his penis plunging into Simone's stretched opening. His organ pushes down, burying itself in Simone's sex, his testicles pressing against her buttocks, the valley between her buttocks, her anus, his penis pulling back now, the length of it pulling out, reappearing, the glans almost revealed, a gathering of white secretion visible at the lower part of Simone's opening. Simone is moaning constantly now. Each time his penis pushes into the depths of her sex, a whimpering cry comes out of her throat. Her eyes remain closed, her mouth open, a sheen of sweat now visible on her forehead.

A kiosk on the edge of the Place de l'Etoile: except for the small rectangular opening that reveals the merchant, the entire front of the kiosk is covered with magazines and newspapers. Two German officers stand facing the kiosk, one of them about to purchase something. This officer wears ordinary officer's trousers. The other officer wears black boots.

The first officer is seen to be carrying a regulation sword at his left side. The names of a number of the magazines and newspapers covering the front of the kiosk are legible: NOTRE COEUR, TRICOT D'ART, MODES D'HIVER, SEMAINE, SIGNAL, ERIKA, NOS ENFANTS, DAS REICH, LA GERBE, DEUT-SCHE ZEITUNG. On the upper part of the kiosk, directly over the heads of the officers, are two guide-books to Paris or maps of Paris, the cover of each showing the Eiffel Tower against a backdrop of the city.

Simone lies on her back on the bed. Quiring is not visible. Simone's eyes are closed. Her right knee is raised, her right foot planted on the edge of the bed. Her left leg hangs over the edge of the bed, the lower part of the leg not visible, but the foot presumably touching the floor. Her right hand lies across the lower part of her left breast, her nipple exposed between her thumb and forefinger. Her left hand is at the joining of her thighs, her palm covering the patch of dark pubic hair, one of her fingertips just touching the shaft of her clitoris.

Quiring's voice is heard: Go on, he says.

No, Simone says. I can't.

Yes, you can. I want you to go on.

From her right side now. Simone is seen from her right side as she lies on the bed on her back. Now her left arm is folded, her right hand supporting her neck as she lifts her head to gaze down at her belly. Her left knee is raised, her right leg extended, her right hand at the joining of her thighs. Now the hand that covers her pubic mound bends, moves, her fingers sliding down to the lips of her sex, her fingers moving, sliding, sliding up again.

She lies back. She rests her head again on the white pillow. Her face is now turned toward her right shoulder, toward the viewer, her eyes closed, her mouth open. Her left hand is now over her right breast, the fingers touching the nipple, rubbing the nipple, circling the nipple, rubbing it again, the wrist of her right hand flexed, bent, the fingers at the lips of her sex, in the groove, out of the groove, and then inside again.

And now she throws her head back. Her mouth is open. No sound is heard. Nothing but silence. Both hands between her thighs now, hands on the insides of her thighs, hands moving inward, fingers at her sex, pressing, pushing, rubbing the hairy mouth as she continues to keep her head thrown back, her eyes closed, her mouth open.

The dining room of the Hotel Prince de Galles in the Avenue Georges V. This hotel is reserved for officers of the German Luftwaffe. The view of the dining room shows two large palm trees, one on the extreme left and the other on the extreme right. In the background, three waiters in white jackets are seen at work at a long serving table. At the extreme left, one waiter is bending forward at a table containing three officers. All the officers of the Luftwaffe are clustered at tables, two or three or four to a table, although in the background at the right one officer appears to be eating alone. The enormous windows of the dining room run from floor to ceiling, the windows perhaps twenty feet high and fifteen feet across. Outside the windows one can see a row of columns on the right and another wing of the hotel is visible in the center. Inside the dining room, each table occupied by German officers has in its center a thin glass vase filled with white and red flowers.

Quiring stands dressed in his uniform, his hands tightening the belt across his chest. Simone lies on the bed with her body covered by the sheet.

You're too modest, Quiring says.

It's awful what you make me do.

I think you like doing it.

I don't know.

Yes, you like it. You're blushing now.

It's awful anyway.

Not with your husband?

Never.

I don't believe it.

But it's true, you know. I've never done that in front of anyone. It's awful.

Then I'm flattered.

Simone sighs: Will you do something for me?

Quiring looks wary: What is it?

Next time I want you to take me while you wear your uniform.

My uniform?

Simone blushes: Yes. You've never done that. I think I want it.

He stares at her. A long moment passes. His face is blank, his eyes fixed on Simone. Then he slowly opens the lower part of his tunic and following that the front of his breeches. He brings his member out. The organ is only half erect but already thickening in his hand. He holds his penis in his hand as he approaches the bed.

In your mouth, Quiring says.

As if in a trance, Simone moves her body until she sits on the edge of the bed with her eyes glued to the pink organ. She finally pushes Quiring's hand away and she takes his penis in her mouth. She sucks at the glans as her fingers curl around the shaft of the organ to stroke it. Quiring has his hands on his hips now, his head bent as he watches her. Simone's eyes are closed, her lips stretched by the thickness of his penis, the fingers of her right hand continually stroking the pink cylinder as she sucks at the front end of it.

Then Quiring mumbles something, pushing his hips forward as his organ begins spurting his liquor in Simone's mouth.

Simone holds her head still until he finishes. A great shudder passes through her body.

*   *   *

A telephone booth in a corner of a metro station. On the wall at the right is a large poster announcing an apparent theatrical entertainment at 58 rue Pigalle. Only part of the title is visible: LA LUNE R——. Below that in smaller letters: LE THEATRE DE NEUF——. The greater area of the poster is occupied by a cartoon-like drawing of a male face with eyeglasses. To the left of the telephone booth is another wall poster, this one advertising a perfume or cologne: EAU DE JAVEL, the small box in the poster showing the letters JAV. The figure in the poster is too obscure to be identified, but it might be the figure of a woman. On the top of the telephone booth is a large sign spanning the width of the booth: TELEPHONE. Two notices are visible on the glass door of the booth, the notices pasted on the glass one above the other, the lower notice with its lower half torn away and missing. On this lower notice only the word ATTENTION is legible. The upper notice contains only three lines, but the lettering is large enough to be completely distinct at some distance: ACCESS FORBIDDEN TO JEWS.

Simone descends the steps into the metro station in the Place St. Augustin. She passes two German soldiers and she avoids their eyes. They look at me, she thinks. They always look at the women. The boys. Even the older ones like Hans. He was so hard today he almost hurt her. Well, what does he want? He wants everything, doesn't he? And he knows she won't refuse. You like it, don't you? Maybe she hates him. Maybe she hates all of them. Do I hate them? The pleasure was never like that, never so much, never like this. It's awful, isn't it? I ought to think about other things. I ought to think about Marie-Claire, not him. She has Marie-Claire to think about. She can still feel it when it's strong like that. She can always feel it for hours and hours. And then of course it's gone and you want more. She feels as if she's caged up, in a cage, an animal in a cage. Each time it's only one emotion. Now she depends on him. She hates it, but it's what she wants, isn't it? It's the same old thing today and tomorrow and the day after that. An embarrassment to think about it. How silly. Darling, you're shocked at yourself. How stupid with him. I ought to cry. It's crazy because she ought to cry and she doesn't want to. She doesn't want to cry, she wants to laugh. That's what she feels and she doesn't know why. She can't depend on anyone so she might as well quit trying. Well, he's strong isn't he? Yes, he's very strong and mean and no good and when she comes she can't stop, it just goes on and on and it's endless. Maybe they can see it in her face, in her eyes. What does she look like? Is it all in one piece again? At least they can tell I'm not a shopgirl with this fur. It's always better to have something that shows what you are. Maybe people ought to wear badges. Maybe the Germans are right about that. Just something to show what you are. She's the

wife of Bernard Duchenne who happens to be quite
successful these days. That's something, isn't it? He
doesn't understand her but it's something. And so I
have my boche. I'm the wife of Bernard Duchenne
and I have my boche. Each to his own boche. But of
course they don't mean it that way, they mean to kill
them. Well, they can't, there are too many, and
anyway it's harmless. It's just something between a
man and a woman and of course nothing changes.

On the Place de l'Opera: the Kommandantur contains the offices of the Kommandant von Gross-Paris.
The tall entrance to the building is situated at the
rounded corner, over the entrance and completely
spanning the curve of the corner the black letters on a
white background: KOMMANDANTUR. And above
the sign, the flagpole extended outward, the swastika, the flag fluttering now in the afternoon breeze
that sweeps down the boulevards from the Seine.
Pedestrians in the open area in front of the
Kommandantur. On the right a long horizontal sign
over a series of ground-level windows: COMPTOIR
NATIONAL D'ESCOMP—the word blocked from
view by a lamppost and a no-parking sign. In the left
foreground, two German officers have their heads
turned to the right, the officer on the far left carrying
a white packet of papers or a box, the other officer's
arms and uniform hidden by a large cape. In the
middle ground, two civilians, a man and a woman,

appear to be crossing each other's paths. And then beyond them another man, his back to the viewer as he proceeds toward the two automobiles parked directly in front of the guarded entrance to the building. The man passes the first car. Then he passes the second car on his way to the guard post, and suddenly it becomes evident the man is Bernard Duchenne.

One of the guards nods at Bernard as he peers at the slip of paper Bernard holds in his hand. The guard gestures at the tall arched entrance. Bernard turns and he walks forward to pass through the arch into the Kommandantur. He has an appointment. This is not a place he would visit without an appointment. He navigates through the crowd in the hall. He finds the stairs, he climbs them, German officers passing him as they come down. Then a corridor, rooms, numbers, finally he arrives.

A German girl, a secretary: Monsieur?

I have an appointment, Bernard says. I have an appointment with Colonel Rademacher. The name is Duchenne.

The girl smiles: Yes, he's waiting for you.

Two well-dressed women walking in the Faubourg St. Honoré, both women wearing coats with large fur collars and small flowered hats tilted forward to almost cover their eyes. One of the women talks while the other listens. They continue to walk slowly toward the rue Royale, one woman talking, the other woman nodding, their collars pulled closed to cover their throats.

Bernard is inside a room with tall windows. The colonel, bareheaded, wearing a dark green tunic festooned with silver braid and a row of three medals, sits behind a large desk.

Sit down, sit down, Colonel Rademacher says. We don't need to be so formal here.

Bernard sits down in a chair opposite the desk: Thank you, Bernard says.

Uniforms, Colonel Rademacher says, a sheet of white paper now held with his two hands, his eyeglasses slipping down on his nose as he gazes at the paper with raised eyebrows. So you want to manufacture uniforms for the Reich, is that it?

And so it begins. Bernard talks. He finds the gray sky outside the windows annoying. He finds Colonel Rademacher annoying. Oberst Rademacher. In German a colonel is an oberst. Damn the Germans, they shouldn't be here anyway. He looks like a baker from Clignancourt. The only thing missing is flour on his nose. The way he rattles that paper. Well, they need uniforms, don't they? They need uniforms and they're better off having them made here where it's cheaper for them. They get everything cheap here anyway. They can get the uniforms, too.

Your contract for the Wermacht blankets is expiring soon?

Yes.

And you want to convert to the production of uniforms.

Yes.

A new contract. Oberst Rademacher shifts his shoulders. Is it a shrug? Oberst Rademacher lifts the telephone receiver, hits the cradle bar with his fingers, jabbers in German, waits, jabbers again, replaces the receiver on the cradle and once again he stares at Bernard.

What does he want? Bernard thinks. Does he want a bribe? No, it can't be. This is the Wermacht and not the Gestapo. They don't take bribes in the Wermacht, everyone in Paris knows it. If he offers a bribe, they may take him into the courtyard and shoot him. Bernard shudders as he imagines himself in front of a firing squad. They do shoot people, don't they? Sometimes he wishes they would do it in public. They could surely find a suitable place for it. Something to see, the ultimate moment, the shooting, the body falling, the soldiers at attention again . . .

Monsieur Duchenne?

Yes? . . . Bernard stares and he suddenly sees the second officer who is now standing beside Oberst Rademacher's desk.

This is Major Sauer, the oberst says. He's the specialist here in military contracts for the Reich.

In the Boulevard des Capucines: an enormous framed poster, a painting of the head of Marshal Pétain, attached to the wall of a building over a display of newspaper pages behind glass. Below the painting of Pétain's head is a banner: THE MARSHAL THANKS THE LEGIONNAIRES FOR THEIR MESSAGE: "IN JOINING THE CRUSADE LED BY GERMANY, THEREBY GAINING THE UNDENIABLE RIGHT TO WORLD GRATITUDE, YOU ARE PLAYING YOUR PART IN WARDING OFF THE BOLSHE-VIK PERIL FROM OUR LAND."

Bernard is now in a cafe in the Avenue de l'Opéra. Is he still trembling? You're an ass, he thinks. You have no reason to be afraid of anything. Didn't he thank you at the end? Didn't he promise to forward the proposal to Berlin? But Bernard is still suspicious. I'm helpless. What can you do with these damn boches? Helpless and frustrated. Thank God Nicole is waiting for him. His fantasy this morning was that Rademacher would make a telephone call and obtain immediate approval. What a ridiculous idea. You're afraid of them, aren't you? Rademacher was all right, but then when the other one came in it was too much, like two wolves, like two animals sniffing around for blood. You're afraid, you ass, you're afraid of something, afraid of them getting you into one of those rooms where they turn the screws on the thumbs, and on the balls. There's a rumor they do it to the balls, too, in the rue des Saussaies. You're afraid, Bernard. I don't like the uniforms. I want to make uniforms for them, but I

don't like their bloody uniforms. But I'll do it. I want
the money. I want the money I want the money.
Where else can you make any money now? And then
when the English surrender and the war is over you
have good contacts in Berlin and everything is fine . . .

On a wall in the rue du Renard: DECREE. In the
course of the past weeks several offenses have been
committed against the lives of members of the German army. In every case, the offenders have been able
to escape. The population has not sufficiently assisted
the attempts to identify and arrest the guilty offenders. As a consequence, I have ordered the following
measures to be applied as of noon on the 20th of
September until noon on the 23rd of September: 1.
All circulation on the public streets is forbidden to
the population in the Department of the Seine between 11 p.m. and 5 a.m. 2. All restaurants, the-
aters, cinemas, and other places of pleasure will be
closed at 10 p.m. 3. During this period, the night
passes now in use will not be valid. A special pass
will be created for persons required by the nature of
their profession not to be displaced after the curfew
hour. The enforcement of this decree will be carried
out by patrols of the German army. Violators who
will be arrested will be considered as hostages. Paris,
19 September 1941. Kommandant von Gross-Paris.

Bernard and Nicole are naked in the flat in the rue

du Ponceau. Nicole is on the low sofa and Bernard kneels on the carpet in front of her. Nicole lies with her head and shoulders against the back of the sofa and her pelvis pushed forward to the edge of the cushion, her left leg raised and resting on Bernard's right shoulder, her right leg pulled away to the side by Bernard's left hand as the cylinder of his penis slowly slides in and out of her stretched anus. Bernard's right hand is on the upper part of Nicole's belly. Nicole's right hand lies on the lower part of her belly, her fingers touching the edge of the triangle of dark pubic hair. Part of a pink silk robe lies draped over the right end of the sofa. The salmon-colored wallpaper behind the sofa shows only a vague pattern

Bernard pushes forward again. You like it, don't you?

It's wicked.

Yes, of course it's wicked, that's why you like it.

He raises her legs now. He pushes her legs up and back toward her face. Nicole helps him by holding the backs of her knees with her hands. Now Nicole closes her eyes and she groans as Bernard pushes his penis forward again. He gazes down at his organ, at the speared opening. He pushes forward another inch, another inch, until finally the bag of his testicles comes to rest against Nicole's buttocks.

Nicole's face: her eyes are still closed. Her mouth opens and her upper teeth become visible. She makes no sound. And then she groans again.

*   *   *

In the rue du Chateau, a corner shop, boulangerie-patisserie, Second Empire colored panels flanking the wide entrance, flanking the windows on each side of the corner. Above the shop, the windows of the house are shuttered. Two German soldiers wearing grey metal helmets now emerge from the shop, one of them carrying a small package, the other with his hands on his belt. They stop at the edge of the sidewalk.

Which way?

To the right.

Are you sure?

Do you want to look at the map?

The hell with the map, let's go.

Bernard is now in a car in the metro again, his eyes on the cover of a magazine held in the hands of an old woman across the aisle. In large letters across the top of the cover is the word SIGNAL. Bernard stares at the letter S. He thinks of Simone. He thinks of Nicole. He thinks of Simone again. He feels more complete with Nicole. Yes, I do, I feel more complete. She lets him do everything and that's more complete. And it's cheap, too. The flat costs hardly anything and she doesn't want much, just a full stomach and some clothes and enough to keep her going. What a sweet little piece she is. She likes you, doesn't she? You can always tell when they really like you. Maybe sometimes they won't admit it even to themselves, but you can always tell. Anyway, she says she does. The way she smiles when she has it inside her. This place or that place, it doesn't matter. She's had everything before, the little bitch. He wasn't the first. But now she's his, does what he wants and always ready. Not like Simone, is she? It's a balance. Every man needs a balance in his life. Simone at home and Nicole in the rue du Ponceau. Peace at home and a bit of fun in the afternoons. We have tricks to do yet, don't we? It's nothing to grumble about. If he had the contract for the uniforms, he wouldn't grumble at all. He'd be happy. Yes, happy. Well, now he feels good. Nicole makes him feel good. Right at this moment, at this very moment he finds himself filled with a sense of optimism about the Germans, about his life, about his daughter, his little girl, the contract, the money, Nicole, the money, the contract, the money, Nicole, the money, the contract . . .

Outside a shop window in the Boulevard Haussmann: a German soldier stands talking to a French woman. The soldier wears a forage cap and he has his back to the viewer. The woman wears a black hat with a brim, a black coat, and black shoes with high heels. She holds a purse under her left arm. Is the soldier talking? The woman smiles. She turns her head to look up the street a moment, and then she turns to look at the soldier again.

*   *   *

Simone and Bernard in the Duchenne sitting room. Bernard has just arrived. He sits down in the armchair opposite Simone as he looks at the mail.

I received a telegram, Simone says.

Bernard looks at her: What?

My Aunt Amelie died.

The old one?

Yes, the old one. I'd like to go to the funeral.

My God.

Yes, I want to go. It's in the Pantin cemetery tomorrow.

What a bother.

It was no bother when your cousin died.

All right, I'll make the arrangements.

Will we go in a car?

No, not a car, we'll use the train.

I'd rather go in a car. Can't you hire a car for the day?

There's no petrol. You can't buy petrol anywhere.

I'm sure you'll find something.

Nicole sits inside the Dome cafe in Montparnasse. She feels comfortable here. Yes, I do. I even like the smell of it. Why is that? Can you figure that out? Onions and sour wine. But after ten minutes you don't smell it any more and it's warm and no one cares what you look like. Bernard of course would never come here. He's not so fancy when he's naked, is he? I'd like to see his wife sometime. Do they do that? Does he do it to her like he does it to me? I want to sleep. I'm so tired now. My mind just runs ahead of things. It's not possible. The way he talks about his little daughter. It's an annoyance, isn't it? I don't want to hear about his little daughter. Why should I want to hear about his little daughter? Next time I'm going to bring a book here and not just a newspaper. I don't like his breath. I really hate him. Yes, I hate him. I hate everything he does. In the front or in the back, it's all the same. I hate him I hate him I hate him . . .

PART TWO: NOVEMBER

A female voice: Nein . . . nicht bestraft werden!

The afternoon sun is blocked by the colonnade and does not reach the interior of the bookshop. Simone stands at the edge of one of the display tables. Outside is the rue de Rivoli, the pedestrians in the colonnade, a German soldier gazing at the shop window.

The clerks in the German bookshop are French. Simone glances at one of the young women. Oh yes, she's French, all right, she certainly couldn't be German. I can always tell when they're French, always tell by the hair and the makeup.

Simone looks down at the books on the table again. The titles are in German. Unreadable. All these books unreadable. I don't know a word of German, Simone thinks. Well, that's not true, is it? She does know a few words. Ja and nein and Heil Hitler and some of the words that Hans uses when he whispers to her. She thinks of Hans. She thinks of

65

the two German officers now standing at the next table. Are they looking at her? Simone imagines she can feel their eyes on her. At the far end of the shop, two ordinary soldiers are chatting with one of the clerks. One of the soldiers has blond hair. Someone is laughing. Simone turns her head to the right, away from the soldiers and the officers.

Then a woman's voice: May I help you, madame?

One of the clerks has approached Simone.

Yes, Simone says. I'd like a book on German military uniforms.

Military uniforms?

Yes, don't you have anything? Something simple? It's for one of my nephews.

In German?

I don't care. I suppose it's the pictures that count.

The young woman smiles and nods and turns away to find something.

Once again Simone imagines the eyes of the two German officers are upon her. She stares at the table again. She feels herself trembling.

In the rue du Ponceau, Nicole lies relaxed on a bed. Seated in a chair near the bed is a man, but the man is not Bernard. The man's name is Lucien and he's Nicole's brother.

Nicole lies with her head and shoulders against the headboard of the bed. She wears a white blouse and over that a dark jacket. Her hair is in disarray. Be-

tween the bed and the chair is a small table supporting a lamp and an ashtray. Behind the bed and the
lamp, the pattern of the wallpaper is visible: vertical
stripes, thin and dark, extending across the entire
wall. As Lucien sits in the upholstered chair, he is
not looking at Nicole. The chair is a few feet forward
of Nicole, so that Lucien sits with part of his back to
Nicole as he stares with fixed eyes at the viewer.
Nicole, however, has her head turned as she gazes at
her brother's back and the side of his face.

When will it be? Nicole says.

Lucien says nothing for a moment, and then he
speaks: Tomorrow. Tomorrow in the afternoon.

Simone walks toward the metro station in the Place
de la Concorde.

A Wermacht motorcyclist zooms around the corner
into the rue Cambon.

Well, what did she think? Simone asks herself.
What did that girl think of it. I don't care. She
doesn't care what the girl in the bookshop thinks.
Now she has what she wants, and something else,
two books. They don't get many French people in
that place. The way she looked at me. I don't care
what she thinks, do I? I really don't. And the officers. One of them looking at my legs. Thank God
I'm wearing the best stockings in Paris. Sometimes
they try to hide the way they look at you. What a pity
Bernard never looks at her like that. He looks at the

young girls in the metro. I've seen him looking. The
big fool. What a big fool he is. My dear Bernard,
you're a big fool. All these years and he's still the
big fool. Walk erect now, keep your back straight.
Almost like an officer. The way they stand so straight
you can't help wondering about things. Makes you
want to see them naked. Do they all smell the same?
No, it's not possible. They can't all smell like Hans.
That would be too ridiculous, wouldn't it? Too ridiculous. Much too ridiculous . . .

What should I wear? Nicole says.
You can wear anything, Lucien says.
I'll wear my raincoat.
I said you can wear anything.
I'll pretend I'm a whore.
Yes, why not? That's a good idea.
It's amusing.
What's amusing?
I'm surprised that you didn't think of it.

Simone is now in the flat in the rue Lavoisier. The
first thing she notices is that the expensive carpets are
gone. The floors are bare in the vestibule and in the
parlor, the exposed wood unpolished and in places
streaked with grime. Well, what's going on? What is
it? She doesn't like waiting. Sometimes she imagines

she hears whispering voices in the flat. It's awful,
isn't it? She never likes waiting for Hans in the flat.
She listens now. Is it a whispering voice or is it just
the wind under the door? She stands near one of the
windows in the sitting room and she prays that Hans
will hurry and arrive the very next moment. As she
thinks of him she now feels the excitement again.
She turns and she looks at the package on the chair
that she brought from the bookshop. The books are
wrapped in ordinary paper and there's no way to tell
that she bought them in that German bookshop in the
rue de Rivoli. She must remember to casually ask
Hans if he's ever visited that bookshop. Yes, I must
ask him. Now as she gazes down into the courtyard,
Simone sees the old concierge limping into the doorway of her tiny kitchen. Well, the concierge ought to
know what happened here, what happened to the
rugs, who these people were and why they're not
here any more. The lamps are so dusty. And I don't
like the old photographs on the walls, the old people,
the eyes, those dark eyes that stare at you. It's too
much. It's really too much. I'll ask Hans to take
them down. I don't want them. We don't need them.
I don't want them . . .

She leaves the sitting room and she walks into the
bedroom. She looks at the shadows in the corners, at
the mirror on the far wall, at the bed, at the gray light
filtered by the curtains, then at the mirror again, at
her face in the mirror. She walks around the bed to
the mirror and she stands before it with her eyes on
her face. Yes, why not? she thinks. As she stands

before the mirror she begins unbuttoning her blouse. She undresses slowly. He'll be amused, won't he? He'll find her naked and he'll be amused. Her fingers work at the buttons as she removes her clothes. She stands in her underwear a moment and she looks at her image again, at her breasts, her belly, her thighs. She takes a deep breath, pulling her stomach in as she turns to look at her profile. Now she quickly removes her brassiere and briefs and she walks to the wardrobe to find something, a robe, a shirt, there must be something in there, anything at all, a robe, yes a robe. She opens the door and she finds a red silk robe. How lovely. A red silk kimono, embroidery. Oh yes I like it, I do like it . . .

What sort of man is he? Lucien says.

Nicole shrugs: His name is Duchenne. He's just a man. There isn't anything unusual about him.

But he's rich.

Yes. Rich enough, anyway. He owns a clothing factory.

My sister and her rich capitalist.

But why not? What do you expect? Do you want me to sleep in the metro?

You could move in with me and Blanche.

The hell with that, I don't want that. You know I don't want that.

*   *   *

Simone is now standing in the sitting room again. She wears the red silk robe as she stands at one of the windows overlooking the courtyard. Almost an hour has passed and Hans hasn't arrived. She gazes down at the courtyard expecting to see his uniform suddenly pass through the gate, but nothing happens, not a soul down there, not even the concierge, no uniform, no Hans, he's not here, he's not coming today, he's not coming, is he? I know he's not coming. I'm alone here. I'm alone in the dust and the silence. He won't come today, he really won't come . . .

Now tell me about tomorrow, Lucien says.

Tell you what? Nicole says. What should I tell you?

Tell me what you're going to do .

You don't trust me.

I want to hear it.

Nicole makes a sound of annoyance: I'm going to the Gestapo building in the rue des Saussaies and I'll stand across the street and wait for Jouvet to come out.

What time?

I'll be there at two o'clock.

And if he doesn't come out at two o'clock?

I'll walk back and forth and wait for him.

Not back and forth. You don't want to be so conspicuous.

Don't worry, they'll think I'm a whore.
Don't be conspicuous.
I'm not an idiot.

Simone is now dressed and out of the flat, walking down the Boulevard Malesherbes toward the Madeleine. She tells herself she won't think of it. This is the first time Hans has failed to arrive at the flat in the rue Lavoisier. No, I won't think of it. It's not true that all the boches are punctual. It's not true. It's not a question of arriving late. He didn't arrive at all. Not at all. He's an officer, isn't he? They have their work, their duties, the Kommandantur, or something unexpected somewhere. You wanted the pleasure, didn't you? I wanted the pleasure. You're an awful girl, aren't you? I ought to buy Marie-Claire a present today, something pretty just to make her smile, to make her laugh. She laughs the way Bernard laughs. She always reminds me of Bernard when she laughs. The way they laugh together, the way they laughed together that time Bernard imitated the boches on the boulevard, one two three four, the way they march, the helmets, the uniforms, the shining buttons, the Germans are here trala lala . . .

And afterward? Lucien says.
After what? Nicole says.
After Jouvet comes out, what do you do?

I walk thirty meters behind him to the Miromesnil metro station.

And then?

When he goes down into the metro, I follow him and I find out whether he takes the first train that comes along or the second train that comes along.

And that's all you do.

It sounds completely stupid.

Lucien sighs: When he gets into the metro, he'll stop somewhere to give you time to get to the platform. He won't look at you. Don't expect him to look at you. Just find out which train he takes.

You think I'm an idiot, don't you?

No, I don't think you're an idiot.

Now near the rue Pasquier Simone sees a small café and she wonders if she ought to rest awhile and collect her thoughts before returning home. Yes, why not? Then as she approaches the entrance to the café, she glances at the window and she sees a woman inside. Their eyes meet. It's Clothilde Ardry, a woman Simone hasn't seen in nearly a year. Clothilde waves at Simone as soon as she enters the café.

Over here, darling, over here. Sit with me. My God, I haven't seen you in so long, last Christmas, wasn't it? Yes, it must be last Christmas.

Simone sits down at the small table. Clothilde has so much amusement in her eyes. When the waiter approaches, Simone orders a pot of tea. Clothilde begins talking, an endless stream of words as she recounts all the difficulties she and her husband Hector have been having in Paris since they decided to return from Nice.

It's horrible, Clothilde says. There's hardly anything to buy any more. They send everything to Germany, don't they? I don't think it's fair. I don't think they ought to treat us like that.

Clothilde's mouth is painted a bright red, the lips working without a stop, and suddenly Simone sees Clothilde's mouth as an aggressive sexual organ and she quivers inside. What a bitch she is, Simone thinks. She looks around them, uneasy because Clothilde continues to talk about the Germans and one never knows who sits in the cafés these days. They always have the Gestapo prying about, don't they?

The waiter brings the pot of tea to Simone.

Well, what have you been up to? Clothilde says. Is Bernard doing well? Yes, of course he's doing well, I can tell by the way you look that he's doing well. Not my Hector, I can tell you that . . . Clothilde leans forward and she whispers at Simone: He's in the gold business, these days. Buying and selling louis . . . Now Clothilde leans back again: What do you think of that? It's ridiculous, isn't it? I don't understand why we had to come back to Paris to struggle like this. Do you understand it? I don't understand it at all . . .

Simone says nothing. She smiles. She stirs her tea.

When will it be over? Clothilde says.

The Germans?

Yes, the Germans.

I don't know, Simone says. Bernard says there's no end to it.

No end to it? That's absurd. It can't go on forever. It just can't.

I don't know, Simone says.

Early evening. Nicole and Lucien are seen leaving the building in the rue du Ponceau. At the edge of the sidewalk, Lucien stops and he looks up and down the deserted street.

I'll see you tomorrow, Lucien says.

At the Flore?

Yes, at the Flore. I'll wait for you.

Simone and Bernard are seated at the dinner table, Simone on the right and Bernard on the left. At the far end of the table, the cook is standing motionless as she watches Bernard reach to the center of the table to lift the salt and pepper carrier. Behind the cook is the buffet and the wide mirror over the buffet in which can be seen the reflection of the table and its white tablecloth.

Now the cook turns and she vanishes to the left. In a moment the door to the dining room is heard to close and Bernard lifts his eyes to Simone:

What did you do this afternoon?

I had tea with Clothilde Ardry.

Clothilde Ardry? Are they back in Paris?

Yes, it seems so.

What's his name?

Hector.

Oh yes, I remember. And what is he doing these days? Did she tell you?

She says he's buying and selling gold.

Bernard chuckles: He'll get caught. Sooner or later they all get caught.

Simone is in Marie-Claire's room, lying on the bed with the girl in her arms, her lips pressed against Marie-Claire's forehead, the young girl smiling as she cuddles against her mother.

Simone kisses her forehead again: Are you sleepy, darling?

Not yet.

What did you do in school today?

I drew a clown.

Was it a nice clown?

Yes, I think so. He had big ears.

Evening at the Moulin Rouge: four women are seen on the steps of the stage, each wearing an elaborate white costume, frilled white lace, feathered hats tilted backward to show their foreheads, the front of each long dress pinned up so that their thighs are exposed,

the dark stockings, the darker bands at the tops of the
stockings, the wide black suspenders attached to the
tops of the stockings. The women are clapping, hands
raised, palms facing each other, the woman at the far
right turning her head to look at the others.

Simone is now in the sitting room with a magazine. She wears a white wool robe. Bernard has
already gone to bed. The sitting room is silent except
for the ticking of the old clock on the mantel. Only
one lamp is lit, the yellow lamp on the small table
beside the chair in which Simone is sitting. Next to
the base of the lamp are the two books that Simone
purchased in the rue de Rivoli. Simone ignores the
books. She turns the pages of the magazine. She
glances at the pictures on each page, a casual glance,
a hesitation, and then the page is turned and the
glance repeated.

In a tomb, she thinks. With the windows covered
because of the blackout, it's like living in a tomb.
It's awful, isn't it? She hates the darkness. Yes, I do
hate it. She feels jittery. What a pity Hans couldn't
be there today. She always feels better after an afternoon with Hans. Yes that's it, it's because Hans
wasn't there, all that waiting and he wasn't there,
waiting naked for him like a stupid goose. You're a
goose, darling, you're a poor little goose. Bernard
couldn't imagine it. He can't imagine anything, can
he? He's in there snoring now, twitching in his sleep

like an old bear. Well, don't think of Bernard. It doesn't do any good to think of Bernard. Think of something else. Clothilde Ardry. How long will it last? she says. Well, I don't know, do I? It might go on for years and years. And that look on her face, those red lips. Dear God, it's really too much . . .

Simone finally puts the magazine into the basket on her right side and she takes one of the books off the small table. She opens the book in her lap and she begins turning the pages.

Uniforms. This is the book about German uniforms. She stops at one double page that shows six men in uniform, three on the left page and three on the right page, the figures carefully drawn and colored, a large swastika flag behind the three men on the left page. Not soldiers. This is not the Wermacht, she knows that. The caption is on the upper left part of the left page. Allgemeine Schutzstaffeln der NSDAP (SS) und SS-Verfugungstruppen (SS-VT). The first man on the left has his hands on his hips. He wears a dark brown kepi, a lighter brown skirt, dark brown breeches, and dark brown boots. The hat shows two insignia: a silver bird with spread wings and below that a silver skull and cross-bones. On his left arm is a swastika armband, the armband red, the swastika black in a white circle, but only part of the swastika visible. A narrow leather belt crosses his chest over his dark brown tie. He stands with his legs apart, and between his boots at the level of his feet is the numeral 1. Simone looks at the small print of the caption: 1. SS-Unterscharfuhrer. She reads the word slowly. She counts the letters. Eighteen letters in all. Don't be absurd, she thinks, it's another language, isn't it? It's not your language, it's the language of the boches. Unterscharfuhrer with his brown shirt and his dark breeches and dark boots. They look so virile, don't they? The belt across his waist, the belt across his chest, his legs wide apart and the two pockets on the sides of the breeches angled and pointing to the seam that runs from his crotch to the buckle of the belt around his waist.

Simone quivers. She wonders if the artist drew the figures from models. This one has such a strong face, a cleft in his chin, the way he stands there with his hands on his hips . . .

2. SS-Oberscharfuhrer. This one stands next to the first man with his arms at his sides. The uniform is black, a peaked cap, a tunic, breeches, boots, leather belts across his chest and waist, all black except the shirt which is brown, the black tie with a red emblem to match the red of the armband on the left sleeve, white trim on the hat, white trim on the two collars, two white stripes near the cuff of the left sleeve. The peaked cap shows two insignia: a silver bird with spread wings and below that a silver skull and cross-bones. He stands with his feet separated by no more than a few inches. He seems relaxed. The face is a bit older than the first one, the jaw strong, the cheek-bones prominent.

Simone holds the book with her left hand, and now she slides her right hand under the book and between her thighs. She wears only a thin nightgown under the robe. She pulls at the hem of the nightgown until her sex is exposed.

3. Rottenfuhrer. Again, the uniform is black. This man wears an overcoat and his body is turned so that he appears in a three-quarter view facing to the left. He wears a peaked black cap that shows two insignia: a silver bird with spread wings and a silver skull and cross-bones. Now the red armband, the black swastika in a white circle, is completely visible on his left sleeve. Attached to the belt at his waist on his left side is a short sword in a scabbard. His left arm is bent, his left hand grasping the hilt of the sword as he gazes at the first two men in uniform. His face is thinner, the cheeks more hollow, his eyes shadowed by the visor of the peaked black cap.

Simone's fingers are touching her sex, her fingertips grazing the hairy cleft, pushing the larger lips aside, one finger probing into the split to find her clitoris.

4. SS-Verfugungstruppen. This uniform is dark green in color and the young man with blond hair stands with his body turned slightly toward the right. He wears a forage cap, a tunic, a wide black belt at his waist, ordinary trousers tucked into black boots that reach only to the mid-calf. Under the dark green tunic, he wears a brown shirt and black tie. The forage cap shows only a silver skull and cross-bones. His hands are relaxed at his sides and there is no sign of an armband on his left sleeve. Like the first man, he has a cleft chin and a strong face.

Simone's hand: the angle of view is from below.

Her fingers are now in the groove of her sex. Her forefinger slowly moves back and forth over the shaft of her clitoris. The other fingers hold the large lips apart. Her fingers are wet, glistening in the dim light. She rubs her clitoris. She slides her fingers between the large lips, the inner lips, down to the mouth of her sex and back to her clitoris again. She teases the curled hairs on either side, pulling at the hairs, twisting them, returning her fingers to the groove again.

5. SS-Sturmbannfuhrer. This man wears a dark green raincoat. His peaked cap is black, the collar of the raincoat black with white trimming at the edges, the buttons of the raincoat silver, his trousers black and his shoes black. The peaked cap shows a silver bird with spread wings and a silver skull and cross-bones. A short sword in a scabbard is attached to his left hip and his left arm is bent as he holds the hilt of the sword with his hand. He faces front, his eyes directed at the viewer, his right hand rigid at his right side.

Simone's face: her eyes are fixed on the open book in her lap. Her mouth is open just enough to show the fullness of her lower lip, her cheeks flushed, her body motionless as she stares at the illustrations of the German uniforms. Now she moves her lips. Her tongue appears, the tip of her tongue sliding over the full lower lip, sliding from right to left before it withdraws into the open mouth. Then an absence of motion again, her eyes now half-closed, her head still bent as she continues to gaze at the book in her lap.

6. Oberfuhrer. This man is in a black uniform. He

stands at the extreme right with his body half turned as he looks down the line at the others. He wears a black or dark grey helmet with a small insignia on the left side, a black swastika in a white circle against a red background. He wears a long black overcoat, a white shirt, a black tie, a black leather belt across his chest, another black belt across his waist, a red armband with a black swastika in a white circle on his left sleeve. His black leather boots are visible below the edge of the overcoat. A closed pistol holster can be seen attached to the waist-belt on the left side.

Simone's hand: her fingers are now moving with more vigor. She continues to stare at the open book with her eyes half-closed. Her forefinger never moves from the shaft of her swollen clitoris. The pink tip of the organ becomes visible each time she pulls the hood upward. Two of the other fingers are now buried in the mouth of her sex, the entire hand moving, the fingers in her sex moving, the forefinger moving on the shaft of her clitoris, her cheeks flushed as now a sudden trembling begins, her thighs closing and opening and closing again . . .

No, Simone thinks. How stupid it is. But you can't help it, can you? How stupid it is to do it like this, here in the sitting room while Bernard sleeps. You're a stupid little girl, darling. You're quite stupid, aren't you? Yes, you're quite stupid. I can't help it. I really can't help it . . .

She closes the book. She takes the second book and she puts the first book in its place on the small table. Now she has the second book in her lap and she opens it. This book is also in German and only two words on the title page have any significance: ADOLF HITLER.

Facing the title page is a black and white photograph of a painting. The Fuhrer Adolf Hitler appears to be standing on a stone monument. Behind him is the silhouette of a large statue of a seated man. The figure behind Hitler is seen from the left side, the left arm extended backward, the right arm forward and the right hand supporting the feet of a large bird with spread wings. In the distant background a building with enormous columns can be seen. In the foreground, the Fuhrer stands with his arms across his front, his right hand grasping his left hand, his left hand holding a peaked cap and what appear to be a pair of gloves. The color of the Fuhrer's uniform is indeterminate because of the nature of the photograph, but Simone guesses it must be brown. Yes, it must be brown like the brown of one of those uniforms she looked at a few moments ago. He wears a white shirt and a dark tie, a thin belt across his chest and a wider belt across his waist. The armband on his left sleeve clearly shows the tilted swastika. He wears breeches and dark boots. He stands with his feet slightly apart and with his eyes directed at the viewer.

Simone is amused by the dark hair combed forward on the left side, the hair forward enough so that it appears to cover his left temple. And the small dark moustache under his nose, brief and square and almost foolish.

But the eyes are not foolish. The Fuhrer's eyes are certainly not foolish. Once again Simone slides her right hand between her thighs. She finds her clitoris and she rubs it. She rubs her clitoris as she gazes at the staring eyes of Adolf Hitler, the Fuhrer, the leader of the Reich, the maker of the New Europe, that man in Berlin, the new force, yes the force in the eyes, I can see it, I can see the force, the strength, oh yes, what a strong face he has, it's marvelous, isn't it? Such determination in the eyes, in the chin, in the way he stands with one hand grasping the other hand, like a monument, like the monument behind him, what a magnificent painting. Does he really look like that? Yes, he does, he does look like that, so noble in the uniform, the boots, the belts, the buttons, the armband, the eyes the eyes the eyes . . .

This is one of the alcoves in the cloakroom of the Sheherazade nightclub. Two shelves above the coatrack are visible, both shelves crammed with German officer caps, ten caps on the top shelf, fifteen caps on the lower shelf. The coat-rack shows a line of hanging overcoats, shoulder-strap insignia in gold and silver, at the far right what appears to be a woman's fur coat. Directly in the center, the hilt of a sword can be seen, the sword apparently attached to one of the overcoats.

Simone sleeps. She lies in the bed beside Bernard

now, curled into a fetal position with her back to
Bernard and the blanket pulled up to her chin to ward
off the chill of the night.

Simone dreams. It's a beach somewhere, the sea in
the background, a gray sky, four figures in the foreground, three women and a man. The male figure is
Adolf Hitler. He sits on a boulder on the right,
completely naked, the upper part of his body turned
toward the sea, his face seen in profile, his left elbow
resting on his right thigh, his right hand on the
boulder behind his back. His body is naked, but his
genitals are hidden by his left thigh, the lower part of
his belly obscure in the shadows.

To the left of Hitler are the three female figures.
The woman at the far left wears a knee length toga
and she holds a spear with both hands, the handle of
the spear digging into the sand of the beach, the tip
of the spear pointing at the sky. She faces the viewer,
her left thigh and leg forward, but her head is turned
and she looks to the right, to the boulder on which
Hitler is seated.

Beside this woman is another woman, this one
completely naked, her back to the viewer, her hair
pinned up in a small chignon above her neck, her
hands holding a large cloth that may be a covering or
a toga recently removed. Her head is bent and she
appears to be staring at the sand of the beach. Her
buttocks are not at all full, more flat than full, even if
her body appears big-boned and solid.

The third woman stands between the second woman
and Hitler. This woman stands facing Hitler with her
right arm raised so that her forearm is positioned

behind her head. Her left arm is extended forward, and over the left forearm is draped either a cloth or a toga, a covering that possibly has just been removed. A patch of dark pubic hair is visible as she stands with her right leg bent slightly at the knee. She looks directly at Hitler as she holds her right forearm behind her head.

Simone stirs in her sleep as she suddenly realizes that she herself is the woman standing naked with her forearm behind her head. But yet it's not possible. She appears to be looking at herself. She does not want to look at herself. She wants to be inside herself. She wants to be the woman who faces Hitler.

The figures remain motionless. Then the figure who is now Simone moves. She slowly drops her right arm, the hand sliding down over her breasts and over her belly and into the patch of dark pubic hair. She gazes directly at Hitler as she pushes her fingers through the curls of dark hair and into the cleft between the larger lips of her sex, between the lips, stroking herself as she continues to gaze at Hitler.

The Fuhrer does not move. His eyes appear vacant. Simone groans in her sleep, a restless groaning before she falls silent again.

The floor show at the Sheherazade: in the background is a wide arc of tables filled with German officers. Several women are visible at the tables, one at the extreme right, one at the extreme left, another

woman in the center but further back in the shadows.
The foreground is occupied by the sole dancer, seen
in profile from her left side, a young woman who
appears in the midst of a turn, a long red skirt split
down the middle, her legs and thighs exposed now as
the two parts of the skirt flare out as she twists her
body. She holds what appears to be a large cape with
her two hands, the cape now floating outward toward
the audience. Above the waist, the woman is naked,
nothing but a small dark covering visible on the tip of
each breast. She does a complete turn now, her body
turning so that she faces the viewer, the two parts of
the skirt flaring outward so that now for the first time
it becomes apparent that under the long skirt she
wears nothing but a cache-sexe, a bright red triangle
that barely covers her pubic mound, the red triangle
appearing and vanishing and appearing again as she
continues to twist and turn and twist to the rhythm of
the loud music. Then suddenly the dancer drops the
cape behind her and her hands are free. She dances to
the right, to the left, and then she slides her hands
over her waist, the two hands meeting at the right
side, the fingers working at the catch that holds the
long skirt in place. Applause now as the skirt is
removed, the woman now whirling again, the tip of
each breast covered by a small dark patch, the pubic
mound covered by the red cloth triangle, the heels of
her black dancing shoes clicking on the scarred wooden
floor. Once again a whirl to the left and a whirl to the
right, her body twisting, the trembling of her breasts
visible, and now she slides a hand over each hip and

suddenly the cache-sexe is removed and the officers
at the tables beginning applauding again, smiling,
nodding at each other, gazing at the dancer again,
gazing at the bared pubic mound, at the prominent
curve of the hairless sex, at the hint of the full slit at
the joining of her white thighs. She dances. She
moves her eyes from one officer to the other. She
continues to dance with her arms extended.

The next day Simone is once again in the flat in
the rue Lavoisier. She stands at one of the windows
in the sitting room with her eyes on the courtyard, on
the narrow gate that opens on the street. Will he
come? Will Hans come today? I won't be foolish
today, not naked today, not like yesterday. How foolish. Such an idiot, darling. Yes, he'll come, won't
he? In a moment she'll see him, his uniform, Hans
moving, walking through the gate and into the courtyard. Well, where is he? There's a smell of soup
coming from somewhere. That stupid concierge with
her prying eyes and long nose. And the others here.
What do they think? Are they frightened by Hans?
Yes of course they are, frightened by Hans and
frightened by me. Yes, why not? He looks important,
doesn't he? He does look important. Oh, what a
pleasure it is. You can't deny it, can you? You can't
deny the pleasure . . .

Simone leaves the window. She's too anxious to
stand there like a mummy waiting for the appearance

of Hans. She walks around the large room and she
finally stops at a picture that hangs on the wall near
the gilt mirror.

The picture is an old framed photograph covered
with glass, an interior scene, a man and a woman and
an infant. On the left is a table supporting a vase
filled with white carnations. Shuttered windows can
be seen in the background. The woman wears a
high-collared old-fashioned dress with puffed sleeves,
a fashion in vogue at the turn of the century. She sits
in a chair, the dress long enough to cover her ankles,
her back erect and her eyes directed at the viewer. In
her lap is a swaddled infant, only the head and arms
of the infant visible, the rest covered by white lace
swaddling that extends down over the lap and knees
of the woman. The infant's head rests on the woman's left forearm. Beside the woman, behind her
right shoulder and between the chair and the vase of
flowers, the man stands with his right hand in the
pocket of his trousers, his left hand behind the woman
and apparently grasping the back of the chair, his
head bent as he gazes down at the infant in the
woman's lap. He wears a dark suit and waistcoat, a
thin chain visible across the front of the waistcoat, the
tip of a white handkerchief in his left breast pocket, a
white shirt with a high collar and a black bow tie.
His face is bearded, a full moustache, a trimmed
beard that touches his tie as he bends his head to gaze
at the child.

Quaint, Simone thinks. Who are they? The people
who once lived in this flat? Or the parents of some-

one who once lived in this flat? Or some relatives of the people who once lived in this flat? It's a mystery, isn't it? Well, this is 1941 and that infant must be as old as Bernard and himself a father standing like this with a wife and child. Then Simone thinks no, these are not the people who lived in this flat, they'd be much too old. I must ask Hans. He certainly knows something, doesn't he? I must ask Hans . . .

Then suddenly she hears a key turning in the lock of the front door of the flat. Oh my God, it's Hans. She turns. She hears the door close. She hears his footsteps in the corridor. She stands there waiting for him. In a moment a uniform fills the doorway of the sitting room.

But it's not Hans.

This man is not Hans.

He's a German officer, all right, but certainly not Hans.

Madame?

Who are you?

He tilts his head: Oberstleutnant Albert Vogel.

Oberstleutnant?

Ah yes. In the French army it would be Lieutenant-Colonel.

But why are you here? Where is Major Quiring?

The oberstleutnant shrugs: Unfortunately, he's been called away.

Called away?

Yes. He suggested you might find me an acceptable substitute.

Simone stares at him.

The oberstleutnant smiles: No? But maybe yes. Why not? These aren't ordinary times, are they?

In the rue des Saussaies a military truck is now passing the entrance to the Gestapo headquarters, the entrance guarded by two sentries, a short line of people at the entrance, another line twenty meters away waiting to approach the first line. Nicole stands at the corner across the road, pacing back and forth, pretending to glance at the windows of the building behind her, the windows, the gates, the bricks, anything at all as she waits for Jouvet. My makeup, Nicole thinks. Well, they think I'm a whore, don't they? They looked at her once and now they don't look at her any more.

Simone and Oberstleutnant Vogel appear only above the waist. Vogel is still dressed, but Simone's blouse has been removed and above her waist she wears only her white brassiere. Vogel stands behind her, his left arm curved around her body so that his left hand lies flat over her diaphragm. Simone's left hand lies above his, her fingers curled around his forefinger as she turns her head to the right so that her chin touches her right shoulder. Vogel's right arm is extended downward and he appears to be holding Simone's right hand with his own. The insignia on his right collar is clearly visible: white, red, and blue stripes in a slanted quadrangle. Vogel leans against her, his left cheek against the back of her head, his mouth against her right temple.

Simone's face: her eyes are lowered, her mouth open slightly. She keeps her face turned toward her right shoulder.

Now Vogel's hands move. He pulls his left hand away from Simone's hand, away from her diaphragm, the hand disappearing around the left side of her body, his right hand now coming into view as it slides upward over her right arm and then backward behind her right shoulder. He keeps his face pressed against the back of her head as his fingers apparently work at the hooks of her brassiere, the hooks in the center of her back. Then suddenly the right side of her brassiere appears to be loose as the brassiere is unhooked, and now Vogel's hands are moving again, sliding over her shoulders to the shoulder-straps, pulling the straps down over her arms, pulling the brassiere away from Simone's breasts. He drops the brassiere, his hands moving upward again to close over her breasts, to hold a breast with each hand so that the nipples are exposed between his thumbs and forefingers.

You're my first woman in France, Vogel says.

Simone sighs: I don't believe it.

But it's true. I arrived from Berlin only a week ago.

Where is Hans?

I had to send him to Holland.

You're his superior officer?

Yes, of course. I thought you knew that. Didn't he tell you?

He told me nothing.

Do you want him back?

It doesn't matter.

Vogel squeezes her breasts: Now you have an oberstleutnant.

Nicole keeps her eyes on the Gestapo building. Then suddenly a small man appears at the entrance, coming out from inside the building. Jouvet. Nicole recognizes him immediately. He has a paper in his hand, and when he hands it to one of the sentries, the soldier looks at it and nods and hands it back to Jouvet. Jouvet makes a right turn and he walks away from the entrance.

Oberstleutnant Vogel is seen in profile from his right side, still dressed, but his tunic has been opened and his breeches lowered to his knees. Simone, seen in profile from her left side, sits before him on a small footstool, her left hand holding his testicles, her right hand holding the shaft of his penis while she licks the underside of his glans. Behind them is an indistinct drapery of some kind, and at the far left, behind Vogel's shoulders, a large white lampshade is visible. Vogel has his hands on his hips, his head bent as he looks down at Simone's face. Simone continues to lick the underside of his glans and now the underside of the shaft of his penis. Her tongue moves up and down. Then she closes her lips over the glans and she holds it in her mouth. The fingers of her left hand lift his testicles. Her lips make a tight ring just behind his glans. Now she pulls her mouth back and the glans is once more visible. Then she slowly engulfs it again, her lips sliding over the swollen flesh, her mouth now pushing further down over the shaft of the penis. Vogel remains motionless. He watches her. Simone's mouth continues to push down, the fingers of her left hand holding his testicles, the fingers of her right hand now at the base of his penis. Her mouth pushes down until it almost reaches the base of his penis, and then it stops and it begins to pull back again.

Jouvet is now in the rue Miromesnil. Nicole has been following him at approximately twenty meters. Once again she notices that Jouvet seems tired. He walks along the wall of the Interior Ministry. Nicole thinks of Lucien. He does think she's an idiot, doesn't he? They wanted her because she knows what Jouvet looks like. She continues walking behind him. Then the entrance to the metro station in the rue la Boetie appears. Jouvet walks into the entrance and vanishes

down the stairs. Nicole curses the cold as she hurries
to follow him.

You're superb, Vogel says.

Simone looks up at him: What did Hans tell you
about me?

He said you have marvelous skin.

Is it true?

Yes.

Take me while you wear your uniform.

Is that what you want?

Yes.

Jouvet has stopped by a poster in the vestibule of
the station. Nicole sees him as soon as she comes
down the stairs. Yes, he's waiting, isn't he? He does
not look at Nicole. He turns from the poster and he
continues on to the platform. He stands and waits.
Nicole trembles as two German soldiers approach
Jouvet. But they ignore him. The soldiers are waiting
for the train like everyone else. Nicole stands back,
her shoulders against the tiled wall, her eyes for
the moment on a telephone booth in the corner of the
station, the sign above the booth: TELEPHONE, the
notice posted on the glass door of the booth: AC-
CESS FORBIDDEN TO JEWS. Then a noise in the
tunnel to the left, the train, the crowd moving for-

ward, the train sliding to a stop along the platform,
the doors opening, people leaving, people entering,
the two soldiers. And Jouvet. He enters one of the
cars and he stands with his back to Nicole. The doors
close. The train begins moving again. Nicole leans
against the poster behind her back. She slides her
hands into the pockets of her coat. She digs into the
pockets to find a piece of black licorice.

Only Simone is seen. She appears to be bending
forward over the edge of a bed, the upper part of her
body flat on the bed, her legs apparently on the floor
at the side of the bed. Her thighs are spread. Her
body is naked and visible only above her thighs, but
at the right the edge of a black stocking can be seen
on the lower part of her right thigh. The angle of
view is slightly from below and directly behind her
buttocks. The plump pubic mound covered with dark
hair is clearly visible, and above that the slit of the
sex, the prominent lips, the end of the slit, the con-
tinuation of the groove and then the whorl of the anus
in the valley between the two buttocks. The dark
curled hair can be seen around the anus, in a thicker
growth along the sides of the large lips, the curls
merging with the hair that covers the pubic mound.
Simone now turns her face to the right and she looks
backward over her right shoulder.

Vogel's voice is heard, but it's no more than a
mumble and the words are indistinct. And then sud-

denly he moves forward, blocking the view of
Simone's buttocks, still wearing his tunic, his breeches
down at his knees and his pale white buttocks now
obscuring everything.

The entrance to the Kommandantur is crowded
again. Sometimes the people pass inward and sometimes the people pass outward. At the next outward
flow of civilians, Bernard emerges. He walks with a
group of pedestrians past the line of cars to the right.
Then he breaks away and he begins crossing the small
square.

His muffler is tight across his throat, the collar of
his overcoat turned up against the chill air.

Well, it's a contract, Bernard thinks. It's a contract, it's a contract. He feels the excitement in his
belly. Of course it's just a small contract, the first
one, but it's a beginning isn't it? Yes, it's a beginning. He's doing uniforms now, maybe a new factory
soon, new suppliers, two thousand SS uniforms. Is it
an honor? Of course, it's an honor, they don't give it
to anyone. Black SS uniforms. The SS man in
Rademacher's office with his patterns. Well, he was
polite, wasn't he? Now a little work to find a good
source of black wool. Only the best, they said. Well,
it won't be easy, will it? But they'll have it. Duchenne
will deliver, won't he? It's a beginning of things, a
new phase. In a few weeks the blankets will be in the
past and uniforms in the future, first two thousand,

then ten thousand, then fifty, and a hundred. How many in the SS, anyway? We'll have all of them wearing a Duchenne uniform at 700 Francs apiece. That's money, isn't it? Yes, that's money, all right. One hundred thousand uniforms at 700 Francs apiece, 70 million and it's just a beginning.

Bernard is now in the metro station. He hates the way it smells these days. They ought to clean it. He opens one of the buttons of his coat. He turns down the collar, moves his shoulders to get himself comfortable. When he turns his head to the right he sees the telephone booth, the sign over the booth, the notices on the windows of the door: ACCESS TO JEWS FORBIDDEN. The platform is crowded, knots of people waiting for the next train. ACCESS TO JEWS FORBIDDEN. It's important to be on the right side, Bernard thinks. He moves to the left on the platform, away from the empty telephone booth. Three German soldiers are talking near a poster advertising something going on in Pigalle. Bernard looks at the uniforms of the soldiers. Good cloth. He knows the quality of a cloth at ten meters. He needs a good pattern-maker now. It's uniforms now. The Germans like the best buttons. Strong thread and the best buttons.

The train arrives. Once again Bernard is annoyed by the smell of the station. He moves with the crowd toward the open doors. All these bodies. Even the

German soldiers are pushing. Well, it's the future, isn't it? Everyone pushing forward into one of the cars. It's the future. It's destiny. That's what the old man says, old Pétain. It's the future and it's destiny.

In the Duchenne sitting room. The shutters are closed and two of the lamps are lit. Simone is seated in an armchair near one of the windows. When Bernard enters, he nods at her:

Well, it's done.

Simone looks up from the magazine she's been reading: What's done?

I've got the contract. Two thousand uniforms for the boches. What do you think of that?

I'm happy for you.

It's a step forward. Two thousand isn't a great deal, but in a month I expect to be up to ten or twenty. And the price is good. They're not cheap, you know.

What kind of uniforms?

The best. Black SS officer uniforms. The best wool. It's a coup, madame. It's quite a coup, isn't it?

Yes, I suppose it is.

Simone puts the magazine on the small table beside her and she rises. She crosses the room to turn on a third lamp. Bernard moves behind her and he leans against her, his chest pressing against her back, his arms circling her waist.

We need to celebrate. Where's Marie-Claire?

She's at the Wepierre house.

Then it's perfect, eh?

The cook is still here.

Never mind the old bitch, she won't bother us.

You're bubbling like a little boy.

Bernard kisses her neck: Yes. Today I'm filled with optimism. We'll have champagne. We'll make a toast to the future.

Simone is amused. She watches Bernard as he hurries away to find some champagne. He returns with a small bottle, smiles at her as he twists the wire. Simone goes to the adjoining dining room and she returns with two glasses. The cork squeaks and pops. Bernard laughs as he fills both glasses.

Oolala, I love champagne in the afternoon . . . Then he puts the bottle down and he lifts his glass: To the new factory.

The new factory?

Yes, of course. I'll get a new factory for this. To the new factory and to the future.

They sip the champagne. Then Bernard puts his glass down on the table and he moves behind Simone again. He kisses her neck, and then he lifts his hands to hold her breasts.

What do you think? Are you happy?

Yes, I'm happy. Don't squeeze me so hard.

Don't you like my hands any more?

Yes, but not now. We can do it later.

He squeezes her breasts again, his fingers digging into the wool of her sweater. He pushes himself against her buttocks, his face against her neck again as he sniffs at her perfume.

Not later, he says. Why not now?

Simone closes her eyes. Does she want it? She feels Bernard pushing against her buttocks, his hands squeezing her breasts through her sweater. She thinks of the uniforms. Black SS uniforms. Dear God. She suddenly imagines Bernard is someone else. It's madness. Who is he? A German officer? Why not? A German SS officer in a black uniform.

In the bedroom, Simone says.

Bernard and Simone are naked on the bed, viewed from the side. The blanket has fallen away and now their bodies are exposed to the unheated air. Simone is seen from her left side, Bernard from his right side. The bedroom door is locked and a small lamp on the night-table is lit, the light hardly illuminating the room, but causing the skin of both Bernard and Simone to take on an orange tinge.

Bernard lies between Simone's thighs. Her legs are raised, her ankles resting on his buttocks. He lies flat against her body, his face pressed against the right side of her neck. Simone's eyes are closed. Her left hand is visible as it lies relaxed below Bernard's right shoulder.

Now Bernard is moving again. He lifts his hips and his penis suddenly appears as it withdraws from Simone's sex. Then he pushes forward again. He mumbles something against her neck. He continues moving. Simone keeps her eyes closed. The rhythm increases and soon Bernard is pushing in and pulling out with a sustained vigor.

And then he pushes forward again, his penis pushing forward into Simone's sex, his hips grinding now, a grunting sound against her neck as she lies there with her eyes closed and her left hand flat on his back below his right shoulder.

Later in the evening. Simone is alone again. She sits in the sitting room in the silence, a wool robe and a book on her lap. Yes, it's Hitler again. She turns the pages. She closes the robe at her throat. It's almost winter, she thinks. Bernard says it will be another cold winter. Then why is my face so warm? Does she have a fever? She looks at the pictures of Hitler. The Fuhrer. She feels it in her sex. Yes, she does. It's ridiculous, of course. Bernard would never understand it. Then she finds a photograph of Hitler with two people that she knows. Oh yes, she does know these people. These are English people. That's the Duke and Duchess of Windsor. Hitler seems to be standing on a pedestal, or on the steps of a building. He has his right arm extended forward, and in his right hand he holds the right hand of the duchess. The duchess is smiling as Hitler bends his head over her hand. Hitler appears to be smiling also. And in the background the duke is staring at Hitler and the duke is also smiling. Everyone is smiling. The duchess wears a small black hat and a black coat. Hitler wears an armband on his left sleeve, and since the left side of his body is turned toward the camera, the tilted swastika on the armband is clearly visible. But these are English, Simone thinks. And now the Germans are fighting the English. She doesn't understand it. No, I don't understand it. Bernard says he understands everything, but I don't understand it. She turns the pages again. Another photograph of Hitler, only his head and shoulders. This time he faces the camera, his eyes directly at the viewer. The shoulder-straps and collar insignia of his uniform are visible. And the eyes. Simone gazes at his eyes. What strength in his eyes. What a marvel it would be to have him look at her. She quivers as she has a sudden fantasy, a room somewhere, Hitler staring at her as she appears naked before him. She feels his eyes on her breasts. She stares at the photograph as she slips her right hand under the book and into her robe and between her thighs. She touches her sex. She finds her clitoris. She stares at Hitler's face as she gives herself pleasure. She keeps her eyes locked on Hitler's eyes as the spasm arrives.

Nicole's brother is once again visiting her in the rue du Ponceau.

Why don't you leave Paris? he says.

Why should I leave? Nicole says. Where do you want me to go?

I can get you papers to cross the line. You can go to Lyon to live with Aunt Lulu.

I don't want to go to Lyon. I don't want to live with Aunt Lulu. You just want to be rid of me.

It's too dangerous for you here.

Why is it too dangerous? I'm not doing anything wrong. I'm just like thousands of other girls in Paris.

It's too dangerous because you're my sister. If they arrest me, they may connect you to me and you'll be arrested, too. You don't want to be arrested, do you?

You didn't think of that when you asked me to follow Jouvet to the metro.

Lucien sighs: We needed someone who knows him. Someone they wouldn't recognize if they were following him. In any case it's over now and nothing happened to you. Let me get you papers for Lyon.

Never.

Nicole, don't be stupid.

I'm not stupid, I can do as I please.

Yes, you do as you please with Duchenne.

You're sneering at me. You shouldn't sneer at me about Duchenne. Here you are in his flat.

It's your flat.

He pays for it, so it's his flat, eh? And now it's past the curfew and that means you're sleeping here again.

Sometimes I have to stay here.

Then don't say anything about Duchenne.

He's a damn collabo.

Nicole waves her arms at him: Everyone in Paris is a damn collabo! What do you think? And anyway I don't care! I don't care, do you hear?

Afternoon. A crowded cafe in the Boulevard de Sebastopol. Bernard has just arrived and now he sits with Nicole at a table near the bar.

We're going to celebrate, Bernard says.

What for?

I got a big contract from Berlin. What do you think of that? Isn't that worth a celebration?

A contract? What kind of a contract?

To make uniforms in a new factory. I thought I told you.

I don't remember.

One hundred thousand uniforms.

My God, that's a lot.

Maybe I'll buy you a fur. Would you like that?

Revillon?

Yes, why not?

In the flat in the rue du Ponceau. The shutters are open in the sitting room, the gray light filtered by the blinds. Bernard and Nicole are standing in the center of the room with their arms around each other as they kiss. Nicole's head is tilted upward, her right hand on the back of Bernard's neck. Bernard's hands move down to Nicole's waist. She opens her eyes and she finally pulls away from him.

Will you really buy me a fur?

Yes.

Do you promise?

Yes. Let's have some champagne.

The empty glasses are waiting on a small table. He uncorks the bottle and he pours the champagne into the two glasses. He hands one of the glasses to Nicole and he raises the other.

To the future, Bernard says. To one hundred thousand uniforms.

Nicole drinks with him: Maybe the war will end, she says.

Bernard laughs: They'll need the uniforms anyway.

Then he puts his glass down and he takes her in his arms again. He kisses her neck, his hands moving down over her back to her buttocks. He squeezes the globes, his fingers pressing through her skirt. When he finally pulls away from her, he lifts the champagne glass and he drains it.

I'm getting drunk, Bernard says.

Nicole nods: If you drink it like that, you will.

You too. Drink with me.

They drink together. Before long, Bernard has her on the sofa. Nicole's skirt is pulled back, her thighs exposed above the tops of her stockings. Bernard runs his hands over her thighs as he leans forward to kiss Nicole's lips. Nicole pulls away and she stands up:

You'll tear my clothes.

Bernard rises and he takes her in his arms again: Don't play the tease now.

He squeezes her buttocks through her skirt. Then he lifts the skirt in back to get at her buttocks through her briefs. Nicole squeals at him when his fingers push into the crack between the two globes. Bernard mumbles something in her ear as he slides his hands up to her breasts, squeezing her breasts, then his right hand down again to slide between her thighs and inside her briefs.

He pushes his fingers inside her sex: You're wet.

Don't be so rough, Nicole says.

You're wet, you little tease. You want it as much as I do.

Only Nicole is seen. She stands beside an upholstered armchair, her back to the viewer, her head turned as she looks back over her right shoulder, her right leg bent, her right knee resting on the arm of the chair, her skirt raised in back to expose her buttocks. Her shoes and stockings have been removed, her buttocks and thighs and legs without any covering.

She gazes at Bernard over her right shoulder: It's cold like this, she says.

Don't move.

It's stupid.

It's not stupid, I like to look at you.

*   *   *

And now on the sofa. Bernard is naked. Nicole is still dressed, but once again her skirt is pushed up to her waist to expose her buttocks and thighs. She lies half-kneeling on the end of the sofa, her left knee on the sofa and her right foot on the floor. Her chin rests on one of the sofa cushions now pushed up at the end of the sofa against the arm. Bernard kneels behind her, his left knee on the sofa, his right foot on the floor directly behind Nicole's right foot. His left hand rests on the back of the sofa while he holds his penis with his right hand. He pushes his organ between Nicole's buttocks.

Not there, she says.

Don't be a fool.

I don't want it there.

Yes, you do. Don't move.

Nicole groans as Bernard pushes his glans inside her anus. He stops a moment. He pushes forward. Nicole groans again. Bernard leans over her back and now he has both hands on the arm of the sofa, his penis pushing inside her anus until nothing is visible except the bag of his testicles pressed against the lips of her sex.

Nicole lifts her head, her eyes closed, her mouth open: Oh God it hurts, she says.

Bernard says nothing. He pulls back, hesitates a moment, and then he pushes forward again.

*   *   *

Sunshine. Noon. The Champs-Elysées.

Simone stands on the edge of the sidewalk near the rue de Berri. The Germans are marching, the soldiers of the garrison of the Kommandant von Gross-Paris, the trumpets, the drums, the banners, the brass of the instruments gleaming in the sun.

She wants to buy a present for Marie-Claire. She gazes at the marching soldiers and she thinks of Marie-Claire. It's guilt, isn't it? Don't be so stupid, you feel guilty, don't you? Yes, why not? you should be home with Marie-Claire, instead here you are watching them again, the uniforms, dear God I don't know, I don't know why I'm here, why am I here? What do these people think? What do they think about when they look at them? That woman who looks at my coat again. I don't care. I don't care if she looks. She ought to be looking at the soldiers. That boy who carries the flag. He's just a boy, isn't he? How many French girls has he had? My God, Simone you're impossible, aren't you? But not with a boy. You don't like the boys do you? There's not enough dignity. Yesterday he made me crazy when he sucked my nipples. Not like Bernard. He's never like Bernard. None of them are ever like Bernard. He's now so happy with his new contract. All these years and he knows nothing except his contracts. But you want it, don't you, darling? You want the comforts. Oh yes you want the comforts. With his uniforms, black uniforms. My God, it's amusing, isn't it? Bernard making black uniforms for the boches. It's enough to make you laugh. They ought to wear black all of them, they would all look better in black. Oh yes, I like the black the best of all. Not like these. The black is the best, isn't it? The black is definitely the best . . .

Bernard is in the Boulevard Malesherbes. He's had a short meeting with a potential supplier of black wool cloth and now he's in the street again when he notices a sudden commotion outside a tobacco shop. Three people seem to be falling over themselves trying to get out of the shop. Bernard stands in the sun and he watches them. Well, it's good to have the sun today, isn't it? He's in good spirits. He feels like walking to his office at the factory, but instead he stands there with several other curious bystanders and he watches the entrance of the tobacco shop. Expecting what? He has no idea. You never know these days. A crowd has gathered. Now signs of a struggle are evident inside the shop. A fracas. An arrest maybe. Yes, it's an arrest of some kind. Two men appear at the entrance, their backs to the sidewalk, one of them holding a pistol in his hand, the other a club, then a third man dragging a fourth man, someone cursing in German. Bernard hears the whispers around him: Gestapo, someone says. The people on the sidewalk begin vanishing, melting away on all sides as Bernard continues to stand there. Yes, it's the police, all right. In a moment a black van pulls up to the edge of the sidewalk. Black, Bernard thinks. That's a good rich black, dense, full-bodied, maybe a bit of blue in it. I'll have to tell Santini to get me a set of swatches, all the blacks, get the wool and colors approved, you can't make a move without approval now. It's too important. Every move needs to be calculated. The man dragged out of the tobacco shop by the Gestapo (not all German please, Bernard is certain at least one of them is French), the man dragged out of the tobacco shop by the Gestapo is now thrown into the interior of the black van only a moment after some of the blood on his head appears on the coat of one of his captors. Captors, yes. He's a prisoner, isn't he? The doors of the van are slammed shut. One of the Gestapo men turns and he stares at Bernard. Bernard stares back at him. I'm not moving, Bernard thinks. They can believe what they want, I'm not moving. If there's any trouble, they can have a word with Colonel Rademacher. But there's no trouble. The Gestapo man turns away, walks to the front of the van and climbs in. In another moment the van is off and away, the exhaust coughing as it rolls down the boulevard, Bernard still standing there, his eyes now on the sidewalk, on the mess. Strange he hadn't noticed it before. All that blood leading from the entrance of the tobacco shop. He hadn't noticed all that blood. Well, that's how it is, isn't it? When things are done in a rush you never notice it all. He has an urge to walk into the tobacco shop and buy something just to see what's going on inside. But he changes his mind. He turns and he begins walking toward the Madeleine.

A gray afternoon and Simone is in the flat in the rue Lavoisier. A Mozart sonata on the phonograph. The shutters are closed in the sitting room, a single yellow lamp throwing a dim light over the furniture. Simone stands with her back to the fireplace, her eyes on the round face of Oberstleutnant Heinrich Muller.

Muller sighs: Do you want me to leave? If you want me to leave, I can understand it. Vogel sometimes presumes too much. Tell me if you want me to leave.

I don't know, Simone says.

You're a beauty.

Thank you.

Vogel and I were in Poland together, you know. He's not a bad sort. He has a sense of humor, doesn't he?

Simone turns away. She doesn't care. In any case she was told by Vogel. He told her next time he would send someone else in his place. Darling, you've become one of their whores, haven't you? No, she doesn't care. He can think what he wants. They can think what they want. She feels his eyes on her. Yes, he can think what he wants. She doesn't care. It doesn't matter and she doesn't care.

I don't mind, Simone says.

Muller is pleased: I brought a present for you.

He goes to the table near the yellow lamp, to the box wrapped in red paper that he brought with him. But then he stops:

No, let's have some wine first. Is there any wine here? I'm from Leipzig, you know. It's the custom to make a toast and drink wine before the present is opened.

Simone leaves the sitting room and she returns with a bottle of red wine. She watches Muller as he carefully uncorks the bottle and pours the wine into two glasses. At least he has clean fingernails, Simone thinks. She takes the wine glass and she waits. Muller recorks the bottle, then he lifts his glass as he gazes at Simone's breasts.

To the unity of the French and German people, Muller says. And to ourselves. To ourselves and to Paris.

PARIS SOIR 21 November 1941: VOL DE NUIT. The poet's bar. Aperitifs. Food. Yolande ROLAND-MICHEL, MICKY. Edgar ROLAND-MICHEL. 8, rue de Colonel -Renard. ETO 41-84.

Oberstleutnant Muller opens the package he has brought for Simone. His gift. He lifts the cover of the white box and he fills his hands with a black peign-

oir, silk stockings, a pair of pink garters. Simone
touches the box. It's from one of the J. Roussel
shops and the lace of the peignoir is extremely fine.

Thank you, Simone says.

I thought you might like black rather than white.

Yes, thank you. I do like black.

I'm pleased.

Would you like me to put them on?

PARIS SOIR 21 November 1941: At the Colisée
and the Madeleine. Zarah Leander. Willy Birgel.
MARIE STUART. The most moving historical evo-
cation. A film by Carl Froelich. ACE. UFA.

Simone is alone in the bedroom, the open box
from the J. Roussel shop on the bed. How quaint he
is, she thinks. A gentleman in uniform from Leipzig.
She gazes at her image in the mirror, at her face, her
eyes, the dark red lipstick that colors her lips. Then
she begins to undress, her sweater, her skirt, her
stockings, the half-slip, the brief girdle she wears in
the cold months, and finally the brassiere. Once again
she gazes at her image in the mirror opposite the bed,
at her breasts, the brown points now responding to
the chill air in the room. Then she reaches for the
white box again. First the stockings and the pink
garters. Well, at least the quality is good. He's not

treating her like a shopgirl. She pulls on the first stocking, then the pink garter, then the second stocking, then the other garter. Then she stands and she slips her feet into the black pumps again. It's fetching, isn't it? The dark silk stockings and pink garters covering her legs while above that her body is white and naked. Now the negligee, a swirl of black lace as she slips it on, as she turns to gaze at the mirror again, a moment of amusement as she notices how the dark pubic thatch below her belly is so completely revealed by the transparency of the fine lace. You're a harlot, Simone thinks. You're a complete harlot.

PARIS SOIR 21 NOVEMBER 1941: AN IMPERISHABLE SOUVENIR available for the Christmas and New Year's holidays. The medal of Marshall PÉTAIN, by the sculptor R. Cochet, is being offered by the jeweler FIX with the collaboration of the medallion engraver Lasserre. On sale at your jeweler at the price of 40 francs. 10% of the proceeds to the National Relief.

And now as she walks into the sitting room again, Simone imagines she's on view in one of the dingy cellars in Pigalle, not one but a few dozen German officers, maybe a general or two, all the eyes upon her, the eyes on the floating peignoir, her legs, her breasts, the dark triangle at the joining of her thighs revealed through the transparent black lace.

Magnificent, Oberstleutnant Muller says . . . He applauds, his pink face beaming as he gazes at Simone . . . You're quite magnificent, he says.

Simone is pleased: Thank you.

She's aware of his eyes. The peignoir hides nothing. When she walks to the small table to lift her wine glass (still half full—she doesn't like red wine that much), she feels Muller's eyes on her buttocks, on the globes that are no doubt revealed, the full derrière that some men find so attractive. And then when she turns to face Muller again, now his eyes are on her breasts, on the dark points of her nipples, on the dark triangle below her belly. She wonders what he thinks. Does he favor blondes or brunettes? Does he find her legs attractive, the dark silk stockings, the pink garters?

More wine? Muller says, his right hand already lifting the wine bottle, holding it out as he offers the wine.

Simone nods. She watches the red wine stream out of the bottle to fill her glass. Like blood, she thinks. The blood red of the wine into the blood red of my body. Just this, just this glass. And I'll feel it, won't I? Just one glass is usually enough, isn't it?

She gazes at his uniform. They stand there facing each other, Muller's eyes on her breasts as she sips the wine in her glass. He compliments her beauty again. He drops his eyes to her belly. Simone enjoys his admiration, the sexual fever in his eyes, the way he's looking at her legs now, the fine stockings, the hot pleasure in his face.

* * *

In the magazine L'ILLUSTRATION: DEUTZ tractors. Loco-tractor. Diesel-Deutz. In all aspects of agriculture and industry, DEUTZ tractors and loco-tractors find their use. KLOCKNER-HUMBOLDT-DEUTZ. A.G. Cologne. Compagnie-Francaise Humboldt-Deutz S.A. 155, Boulevard Haussmann, Paris-8e. Tel.: BALsac 03-12 to 03-16.

Oberstleutnant Muller has placed his right hand on Simone's shoulder. She feels the warmth of his hand through the thin lace of the peignoir. She remains motionless, her eyes on his face, on his chin, on the faint dueling scar on his left cheek. Muller's eyes are on her breasts. He drops his hand now, his right hand sliding down over her left breast, holding the globe of the breast through the silk and lace of the peignoir. Then he moves his hand again, he steps to the side, his right hand slipping down over Simone's left hip and around to the curve of her left buttock. Simone quivers as she feels his fingers pressing into her flesh, his right hand fondling her left buttock as his left hand now touches her belly, sliding over her belly while he keeps his body apart from hers. Only the hands. One hand on her left buttock, the other hand on her belly, each hand moving slowly, dragging the lace over the smooth skin underneath it.

Simone trembles. She sees the sweat on Muller's forehead, the red blotch on his cheek just under his dueling scar. She wonders what he would be without the Wermacht. A businessman like her husband? A teacher? A streetcar conductor? Oberstleutnant Heinrich Muller might be a clerk in a Leipzig bank. Yes, why not a clerk? A clerk in a Wermacht uniform. Simone studies the buttons, the braid, the collar insignia, the speck of lint just over the embroidered bird with spread wings on the right side of his chest. Then she drops her eyes and she looks at the front of his breeches. Is he aroused? Simone trembles again. Muller is touching her right breast now, his fingers rubbing the nipple through the lace.

Then he steps back, his cheeks flushed as he gazes at her: Vogel told me how much you like our uniforms.

Yes, I do, Simone says.

Muller tilts his head. Is he smiling? He straightens up a moment, holds himself erect in his uniform, his tunic belted at the waist, his breeches, his boots. Then his hands move to the lower part of his tunic, opening the tunic on each side to get at the front of his breeches.

Simone watches it. She blushes. Muller's fingers work at the fly of his breeches, his fingers sliding inside the opening to extract a limp penis, a long member, then the opening in his breeches made wider and his testicles brought out, the long penis dangling over the pink sac.

This is what you do with Vogel, isn't it? He wears his uniform.

Yes, Simone says.

In the magazine L'ILLUSTRATION: GIBBS for your hygiene. GIBBS for your elegance. GIBBS for your economy.

Muller is now leaning against the wall. His belt has been removed. He uses both hands to pull the lower part of his tunic away from the front of his breeches. He bends his head as he looks down at Simone. She sits on a small footstool in front of Muller, her right hand on his knee directly above the top of his boot, her left hand holding his testicles and the lower part of his penis, her mouth open, her tongue slowly licking the bulb of his glans.

Simone's mouth: the edges of her teeth are visible. Her tongue continues to move back and forth over the tip of the penis.

In the magazine L'ILLUSTRATION: UNIC the perfect fountain pen. The "UNIC" fountain pen is elegant, sober, modern, and sold with the guarantee of the manufacturer.

Oberstleutnant Muller has Simone on the bed. The peignoir has been removed. She kneels on the edge of the bed on all fours, her head down, her face turned as she looks back over her left shoulder. Her left breast is visible as it hangs toward the yellow counterpane. She wears the dark stockings, the pink garters. Muller still wears his uniform. He stands behind Simone's buttocks, his penis and testicles protruding from the opening in his breeches, his hands on the upper slopes of Simone's buttocks, the glans of his penis just entering between the hairy lips of Simone's sex.

Muller pushes forward. The glans vanishes into the entry. He continues to push forward until the sac of his testicles presses against the lower part of Simone's sex, the bulging pads of the outer lips, the curled dark hair that grows more profusely at the slit and further down around the clitoris.

Then he pulls back. More quickly now. He pulls back until only the glans is still hidden. He pushes forward again. He pulls back. Forward and back, forward and back, forward and back.

Simone continues to look backward over her left shoulder. Now she closes her eyes. She opens them again. Muller continues to stroke his penis in and out of the mouth of her sex.

Then he suddenly pulls himself free: In your mouth, he says.

For a moment Simone is stunned by the sudden withdrawal. Then she moves, her body shifting, turning until she sits on the edge of the bed in front of Muller. She takes his swollen member in her right hand, but as she opens her mouth the white sperm

suddenly begins to spurt from the tip. Muller groans
as the second jet of sperm strikes Simone's left cheek.
She takes him with her mouth, her lips sliding over
the spurting penis, her fingers stroking it, her eyes
closed as Muller makes another sound in his throat.

Holy God, Muller says.

Simone pulls her mouth off the long member and
she begins to lick the tip of it again.

In front of the Cinema Imperial in the Boulevard
des Italiens: THE ACROBAT on the marquee. Pedestrians on the pavement in front of the entrance.
Three German soldiers are walking to the left, one
German officer is walking to the right. The officer
has his right hand raised in a salute, apparently in
response to the salute of one of the soldiers. Five
civilians can be seen on the sidewalk, three men and
two women, one of the women with her head turned
as she looks directly at the entrance to the theater.
The man at the left, directly in front of the three
soldiers, carries a wrapped package in the crook of
his left arm. He wears a black muffler that covers the
lower part of his face, but now he pulls the muffler
down and for the first time he can be recognized as
Lucien.

Afternoon in a café in the rue Feydeau. Bernard is

with a man called Giroud, seated at a table in a corner, Bernard with his back against the wall and his eyes on the crowd. He has a cup of ersatz coffee in front of him, the cup still half full, the bitter taste of the coffee still on his tongue. Giroud is now smoking his third cigarette. He sits opposite Bernard with his eyes on Bernard's wristwatch. Giroud's face is pale, a pasty white color at his temples and around his chin. Only his nose shows any sign of life, any sign of blood flowing under the skin. He appears restless. Now he moves his eyes from Bernard's watch to Bernard's face.

Well, what do you think? Giroud says. It's a good offer.

Bernard shrugs: I don't want any gold.

Giroud rolls his eyes: Are you sure? Everyone wants gold these days. I thought of you because we're friends. It's not only an investment, you know. It's insurance. No matter what happens, the gold is always worth something.

Bernard looks at him. Giroud's fingernails are bitten to the quick and not at all clean. He's a beggar, Bernard thinks. He smiles at Giroud. He doesn't have long, Bernard thinks. The man will soon be in rags. Either here in Paris or in a camp somewhere.

I'm not doing anything with gold, Bernard says. I don't need any gold.

Why not?

The only people who want gold are the people who want to get out. I'm not getting out, you see. I'm not going anywhere.

Giroud sighs: I've been very busy these days. I've bought and sold millions.

Listen, I'm not interested.

Giroud says nothing. The crowd is noisy again, the noise drowning out the cough that now comes out of Giroud's throat. Bernard feels a momentary pity for the man. He peers though the smoke at Giroud's pale face. Is he sick? Yes, he must be sick. He looks on the edge of death, doesn't he?

Why don't you change your mind? Giroud says.

I'm not interested.

Giroud twists his lips with annoyance. Then he looks away and he puffs at his cigarette again.

Bernard is now walking in the rue du Ponceau. Except for a small dog shivering in the doorway of a closed bakery, the narrow street is deserted. Bernard approaches the entrance of No.4. He pushes the glass door open and he steps inside the dark vestibule. He pushes another door open and now he's at the bottom of the stairs. He begins climbing, his eyes on the shadows, on the dim yellow light on the first landing. Then he hears a noise above. Someone is coming down. The noise of feet on the stairs becomes gradually louder as Bernard continues to climb. Finally he sees a man descending. As they draw closer, Bernard nods but the man ignores him. They pass each other just below the third floor. Bernard continues climbing. He turns to glance down the stairwell at the other man. He hears the vestibule door downstairs rattle as the man closes it. Unfriendly bastard, Bernard thinks. You never know who lives next door to you. Well, you don't live here do you? Nicole lives here and not you. The hell with it, I don't care. Sooner or later they get theirs and I don't care.

In a moment Bernard is knocking at the door of Nicole's flat, the door opening, Nicole looking at him with amazed eyes before she opens her mouth.

It's you.

Bernard steps inside the flat: Who else?

I didn't expect you.

Why not? I told you I'd be here at two o'clock.

I forgot.

She smiles at him now. Bernard wonders if she seems agitated. She's not that old, is she? At her age they tend to get agitated. He walks into the sitting room and Nicole follows him. Then he decides he wants some mineral water and he turns back to the kitchen alone. But inside the small kitchen he notices the two wine glasses on the board and he forgets about the mineral water. Never mind the mineral water, why two glasses here? Two empty wine glasses. Bernard stares at them. He thinks of the man he passed on the stairs. Is it possible? Yes, of course it's possible. I wouldn't be the first, Bernard thinks. It's possible and I wouldn't be the first, would I?

He walks into the sitting room again. The shutters are open and the gray afternoon sky can be seen through the windows. Nicole approaches Bernard, leaning against him as she kisses him.

I'm happy you're here, Nicole says.

She kisses him again, her lips pressing against his. Bernard says nothing. He wants to avoid conflict. He slips an arm around her waist and he pats her buttocks. No questions, he thinks. She's not the sort to keep her head, is she? Then he pulls his arm away and he sits down on the sofa.

Would you like some tea? Nicole says. I was just about to make some for myself.

Bernard nods: Good idea.

He watches her as she walks to the kitchen. He watches her legs. Yes, he likes her, he does like her. She's not as difficult as the last one. This time he made certain it wouldn't be one of the girls at the factory. The fact is, Nicole sometimes reminds him of Simone. Yes, she does. She does remind him of Simone. It's good that she's young, isn't it? It's much better when they're young. Oh yes, it's much better.

After a while Nicole returns with two cups of tea on a tray. She puts the tray down on a small table. She hands one of the teacups to Bernard. She gazes at him.

Nicole's face: her head is turned slightly to the side, her eyes looking down at the teacup in her hand and then up at Bernard's face again.

I don't have enough money, Nicole says.

Bernard stares at her: What?

Everything is so expensive now and I don't have enough money. I don't know what to do.

How much do you need?

I don't know. I want to buy clothes. I need new stockings. How long will the occupation last?

Bernard sighs: No one knows that.

Will it go on forever?

Maybe it will.

I don't like the boches.

They're not much different than we are.

I don't like them.

How much money do you need?

I don't know.

I'll give you two thousand francs. Will that be enough?

Yes, I think so. It's cold, isn't it? I hate the cold weather.

Bernard says nothing. He sips his tea as he gazes at her breasts. The grey sweater she wears is tight enough to show everything.

Lucien is now in a café, maybe in the rue du Helder. He sits at a table with another man, and at the moment he is seen on the left with his right arm extended as he lights the other man's cigarette with a cigarette lighter. When the cigarette is lit, Lucien snaps the lighter closed and he withdraws his hand back to his lap.

How soon will it be? Lucien says.

The other man shrugs: I don't know, maybe a week.

Three days.

Listen, it's not so easy in three days.

Three days.

All right, I'll try. I can't promise anything, but I'll try just for you.

Bernard and Nicole are still on the sofa, but Nicole is now lying across his lap. She lies on her left side, her left hand on his left knee, her right arm raised as she strokes his neck with her right hand. Her head is lifted, her eyes closed, her mouth open as Bernard bends forward to press his face against her hair. Bernard's right hand is on her hip, and now the hand moves, sliding to the right toward Nicole's waist, sliding further until it comes to rest on her sweater over her right breast.

His face moves and he kisses her open mouth. His hand fondles her breast, then slides back again to her hip and down to her right thigh. He rubs her thigh, his fingers pushing at the edge of her skirt, sliding over the top of her stocking to find the bare skin.

He pulls his mouth away and he gazes down at her: Why don't you suck me?

Nicole says nothing for a moment: Let's go to the bedroom.

No, do it here. I can't stay long. I've got to get back.

She moves her body and she sits up on the sofa beside him. Then she mumbles something as she slides down to kneel on the carpet between his legs.

Bernard has already opened the top of his trousers, and now he unbuttons his fly and he pulls his hands away. Nicole uses both hands to bring his organ out of the opening in his trousers. His penis is only half erect, the glans still covered by the foreskin. Nicole pushes the foreskin back with her fingers and she begins licking the exposed glans as Bernard watches her.

In the magazine L'ILLUSTRATION: Nice. HOTEL ROYAL. Promenade des Anglais. International reputation. Open all year. Nice. Hotel RUHL. The best location on the Promenade des Anglais. Open all year. The Nice hotels AMBASSADOR and O'CONNOR and their restaurant and gardens are open.

Bernard's penis is in Nicole's mouth. The erection is much stronger now, the thickness of the organ visibly stretching her lips. She moves her head up and down, her lips sliding halfway down to the base of his penis and then pulling back again. She repeats the movement several times, and then she pulls her mouth away and she licks the tip of the glans with her tongue.

Bernard's pleasure is evident in his face. His head is bent as he watches Nicole. Then he makes a sound in his throat and he opens his mouth. Nicole has now closed her lips over the glans of his penis, and she holds her mouth there as Bernard begins to groan again. He closes his eyes and he throws his head back as he continues to ejaculate. Nicole holds the glans in her mouth until he's finished. Then she rises without looking at him and she walks toward the kitchen.

Eleven o'clock at night in the Duchenne bedroom. Only a small lamp is lit. Simone lies under the blanket on the right side of the bed, flat on her back with her eyes open. Bernard now appears near the left side of the bed. He wears light blue pajamas and he has a toothbrush in his mouth. He removes the toothbrush from his mouth and he speaks to Simone:

What about Sunday? We can take the kid to the zoo on Sunday. Would you like that?

Simone turns her head and she looks at him: Yes, why not?

Late morning in the Duchenne flat. Simone is alone, seated in an armchair near one of the windows. She holds a magazine in her lap, but she's not reading it. She gazes directly at the viewer, her face empty of any expression. There is no sound in the room, nothing but a faint murmur that might be a truck or a motorcycle in a street somewhere.

This morning after breakfast she suddenly felt guilty about everything. She feels it again now. She slides her hands forward over the magazine and she takes hold of her knees. My affairs, she thinks. All my affairs. She thinks of the flat in the rue Lavoisier. The German officers. The uniforms. There have been two more since Muller. How many does that make? I don't want to think of it. But she can't help it. She thinks of herself naked in the rue Lavoisier, naked in the sitting room, naked in the bedroom, the uniforms, the boots. How many times now has she been taken while they wear their boots? It's too much, it's really too much. They're not all the same, are they? The smell is different, the hands, the eyes, the mouth, everything is different with each one. You're a whore, darling. No, I'm not a whore. I don't take any money do I? Then what am I? There must be a name for it. What should I call myself? I don't know the names any more, all the boche names. I don't know them. I don't know any of them. It goes on and on. She never knows who will show up at the flat in the rue Lavoisier. She has no idea who pays the rent for the flat. I don't know. I don't know anything, do I? It's absurd, isn't it? I don't know anything . . .

Suddenly the doorbell rings. Simone is startled. She does nothing for a moment. She sits there and she stares at the entrance to the sitting room. Who can it be? She's not expecting anyone. She's annoyed that the maid is out. Then finally Simone rises and she leaves the sitting room. She walks down the corridor to the front door of the flat, and just as she

approaches the door the bell rings again. The harsh
sound of it irritates Simone. She hesitates a moment,
and then at last she unlocks the door and she opens
it.

A woman stands at the entrance. It's Clothilde
Ardry. Simone stares blankly at her a moment before
she speaks: Clothilde.

Clothilde tosses her head: Well, thank God you're
home. For a moment I thought you might be out.
May I come in?

Simone stares at Clothilde's red mouth, and then
she abruptly moves out of the way: Yes, of course.
Please come inside.

They sit facing each other in the sitting room.
Clothilde is talking. She wears a dark blue dress,
brown stockings, and dark blue shoes. Simone hardly
hears the words. She wonders why she's annoyed.
She tells herself she'd rather be alone. How strange
that Clothilde Ardry has come to visit her. But you
must show some hospitality, Simone thinks.

Would you like some tea? Simone says.

Clothilde stops talking, and then she shrugs: Yes,
but later. I want to talk to you first.

So Simone listens again. Well, it's not the first
time, is it? Clothilde has been here before. Simone
watches Clothilde's hands as Clothilde continues talking. Clothilde's fingernails are painted a bright red.
Her eyes dance as she talks. What does she want?

Simone thinks. She wonders if Clothilde's jewels are fake. Is she in trouble? Clothilde seems nervous, more hysterical than usual.

I need a favor from you, Clothilde says.

A favor?

Do you mind?

What is it?

Clothilde sighs: It's about Hector.

Simone hesitates: I don't think Bernard is interested in gold these days.

It's not about gold. Hector has been arrested.

Oh dear. Is it the gold?

No, it's petrol. I wish it was gold. I think if they'd caught him selling gold they'd be easier on him.

Dear Clothilde, I'm so sorry.

Poor Hector, Simone thinks. How awful to be arrested. She remembers now what Bernard said. Bernard was certain that Hector would sooner or later be arrested for dealing on the black market. Clothilde is talking again. Simone watches Clothilde's eyes as Clothilde talks. What is she saying? She does seem disturbed, doesn't she? What will Bernard say? Simone is suddenly thankful that Bernard is not Hector. But of course Bernard could never be Hector, could he?

Bernard knows people, Clothilde says.

Simone looks at her: He knows people?

Yes, you know that. He knows all sorts of people, doesn't he?

Simone gazes at Clothilde's dress again. She decides the color of the dress is awful. The shoes aren't bad, but the dress is awful.

He has influence, Clothilde says. It's not as if Hector is a spy, is it? Bernard must have some influence with the Gestapo. If someone doesn't do something, they'll send Hector to prison, won't they?

Or worse, Simone thinks. They might shoot him.

I thought Bernard might do something, Clothilde says. He's Hector's friend, isn't he? I mean they've known each other such a long time.

Simone shifts her body in her chair. It's too much, she thinks. It's completely absurd, isn't it? Then she speaks to Clothilde again: Would you like some tea now?

After Clothilde leaves, Simone returns to the sitting room and she sits down again. She picks out one of the magazines from the basket beside the chair and she begins turning the pages without really looking at anything. She thinks of Clothilde. She thinks of Hector. Has he really been arrested by the Gestapo? Well, you know it must be true, Simone thinks. Then she sees an advertisement for children's games. LES JEUX WITHO. Games by Witho. Directing the youth of France toward the ideal of duty. Conceived and realized under the emblem WORK, FAMILY, FATHERLAND. The Game of Obstacles. The Game of the History of France. The Game of the Treasures of France. The Three Colors. Matho, Odyssey of a Nomad Soldier. The Trumps of Life. Ten Manly Weapons presented by Ten Great French Figures. WITHO games educate and instruct in happiness. On sale: department stores, bookshops, toy stores. Wholesale: WITHO, 51, rue de Paradis, Paris 10e. PRO 28-05.

Something for Marie-Claire, Simone thinks. The Game of the History of France. Yes, why not? She might like it. I'll buy it for her. But then Simone remembers that she planned to go to the rue Lavoisier today. So now she thinks of the flat in the rue Lavoisier, the officers, the uniforms, the bed and what clothes she ought to wear and who it will be today. Will it be Muller again? You're trembling, darling. Yes, you're trembling, aren't you? Well, I can buy the present for Marie-Claire afterward, can't I? A child needs a proper upbringing, a WITHO game directed toward the ideal of duty, WORK, FAMILY, FATHERLAND. Hector Ardry ought to have known better. Do you feel sorry for Clothilde? Yes, I do feel sorry for the poor woman. It must be awful for her. But she carries it well, doesn't she? She does carry it well. Oh, never mind. I'm sure Marie-Claire will be delighted with one of these interesting little games. Or maybe two. Yes two. I'll buy her two games. What a fine idea. Two games to make it certain that she likes at least one of them. Two games after the rue Lavoisier. Two games for Marie-Claire . . .

Vertical shadows and the sound of machines. Sewing machines. Only one machine at first, the needle moving up and down as it repetitively stabs a field of black cloth. Now a woman's hands appear, the fingers guiding the cloth under the moving needle.

This is Bernard's factory. In view now is a long line of sewing machines, each machine tended by a woman, her hands on the machine table, her fingers pushing black cloth under the moving needle. Twenty workers can be seen. At the far right, in the background, is an office with glass walls. As the office is approached, Bernard can be seen behind his desk. He has a pencil in one hand and in the other hand he holds a sheet of yellow paper. Now he makes a mark on the yellow paper with his pencil.

He glances through the glass at the workers in the large area outside the office. Twenty uniforms a day. It's too slow, isn't it? You ought to do fifty or a hundred. Get a larger place. But then what happens if they don't give me another contract? One can't sell SS uniforms on the street, can one? Ha ha. And he doesn't like this office. He doesn't like looking at them out there, his little robots. He ought to leave here now and go to Nicole. It's better to think of Nicole, isn't it? That hard little rear she has. Does she have a lover? It's an annoyance, he thinks. He doesn't want to think of it. I don't want to think of it. Maybe she does have a lover, someone else beside himself. Maybe she gets money from both of us. She's a clever little whore, isn't she? You think you have something private and then you find out it's not private at all, you're not the only one, you're just another one in there, just another fool . . .

One of the women at the machines rises now, and

she turns and she begins walking toward the office.
Bernard watches her as she approaches the open
door. He tries to remember her name. Is it Eva?
She's a new one, isn't she? She has a pretty face, a
sturdy body, strong legs.

Monsieur Duchenne?

Yes?

I can't work this afternoon. I have to go to the
hospital.

Is someone sick?

My husband.

When will you go?

In an hour.

Don't forget to clean your machine.

Bernard watches her buttocks as she turns away.
Peasant stock, he thinks. She must be thirty. A woman
with a solid body. He amuses himself by imagining her
naked. Then he feels a sudden lust for Nicole. Dear
God, it's not even two o'clock. He stares at the
machines. He watches Eva as she sits down at her
machine and begins to work again. Is her name really
Eva? She must have magnificent breasts. Then as he
gazes at her, Eva turns her head and she glances at
him. A long glance from Eva's dark eyes. Bernard
thinks of Nicole again and he decides to visit her.
He'll buy her a present and surprise her with it. He
looks at his desk. Then he looks at Eva again and
once more he finds her looking back at him. Now
Bernard is amused. He wouldn't mind it, would he?
But no, not here. Never again with one of these

women. You have Nicole, don't you? You have the
flat in the rue du Ponceau . . .

Nicole lies on the sofa in the sitting room in the
flat in the rue du Ponceau. She is seen from her right
side, her body extended on the sofa, her head resting
on a pillow propped against one of the arms of the
sofa. In her right hand she holds a half-filled glass of
white wine. Lucien sits in an armchair at the right,
his back erect, his eyes on his sister.

Nicole's face: her lips are drawn in and she appears
annoyed at something.

I don't want any trouble with him, Nicole says.

For a moment, Lucien says nothing. Then he speaks:
Don't be absurd.

I tell you I don't want any trouble with him.

What do you suggest? Are you telling me not to
come here any more?

I just don't want any trouble with him.

All right, I won't come here any more.

You can come in the evening, can't you? He never
comes here in the evening because of his wife.

What do you know about her?

I don't know anything about her and I don't care.

Then you don't love him.

My God, you're crazy. I never said I loved him.
Did I ever say that?

Nicole continues talking. Lucien listens and he

says nothing. Nicole's voice gradually becomes more and more indistinct. Lucien finally rises and he walks to one of the windows. He stands near the curtain with his eyes on the street.

Are they looking for you? Nicole says.

I don't know.

What happens when they arrest you?

What happens? I don't know what happens. Everything goes on as usual, I suppose.

No, I mean what will they do to you?

They'll try to make me talk.

And will you?

I don't know. I don't think so.

What do they do?

It's too ugly. I don't want to talk about it.

Nicole laughs: I know they torture people.

I don't want to talk about it.

They'll arrest you and they'll torture you.

I tell you I don't want to talk about it.

Lucien now removes a package of cigarettes from one of the pockets of his jacket. He puts a cigarette in his mouth and he lights it with his cigarette lighter.

Don't you have any work for me? Nicole says.

What do you mean?

You know what I mean. Don't you want me to follow someone?

Don't make a joke of it.

I'm serious. I don't mind doing it.

It's too dangerous.

I said I don't mind it. Maybe I could do something indoors. I hate the cold weather.

Lucien sighs. He returns to the armchair and he sits down again. He takes another puff of the cigarette and then he looks at Nicole:

How much money does he give you?

Not very much.

You could get a job, you know.

I don't want a stupid job.

There's no future for you in Paris.

Why not? Everyone is here.

The Germans are here, too.

So what? Everything is the same, isn't it? I don't care about the Germans.

Everything is not the same. They arrest people and they shoot them. Why don't you leave? I can get you a pass to cross the border. You can go to Marseilles.

I don't want to go to Marseilles. Take me to the cinema.

What?

Take me to the cinema. We can see Marie Stuart at the Colisée.

You're crazy. Is that all you can think about?

You want me to leave Paris because of Bernard.

I want you to leave because it's dangerous here.

You think I'm a whore.

I don't care about him. Why don't you leave? Why don't you be sensible? It's very dangerous here.

I don't care. I don't mind it. I have this flat and I'm not leaving it.

*   *   *

Simone has just entered the courtyard of the building in the rue Lavoisier. She ignores the lighted window of the concierge's apartment, and she crosses the courtyard to the heavy wooden door. This door is never locked and it swings open easily after the doorknob is turned. She opens the inner door with a key and then she begins climbing the stairs.

Are you eager, darling? Simone quivers as she asks herself the question. Yes, why not? After that awful time with Clothilde Ardry, she deserves something now.

She finishes climbing the stairs to the door of the flat. She unlocks the door and opens it and enters the flat, and in a moment the smell of cigarette smoke informs her that she's not alone.

Is it Muller? Who is it this time? Simone feels the heat in her face as she walks down the hall to the sitting room, as she stands in the open doorway. The man standing at the window now turns to look at her. He's not anyone she knows. A new man. A new officer. He draws himself erect, the heels of his boots together as he gives a short bow with his head:

Madame Duchenne?

Simone nods, but she does not enter the sitting room: Yes.

I am Colonel Albert Kremer. Oberst Albert Kremer.

Simone says nothing. She hesitates a moment, then finally she enters the sitting room. She avoids his eyes as she begins removing her hat and coat.

The colonel does nothing. He stands there and he watches her. After the coat and hat are deposited on one of the armchairs, Simone turns around and she faces him. She looks down at his boots and then up at his eyes again. Is he amused? She sees the arrogance in his eyes and she suddenly begins to tremble.

I must say I'm surprised, Kremer says. Muller's description was less than satisfactory. He underestimates your beauty

Simone avoids his eyes again: Thank you.

Now Kremer turns away and he begins talking. He talks about the flat. Jewish communists, he says. Do you find it comfortable?

I don't live here, Simone says.

Yes, I know. You live in the rue Therese and your husband has a contract with the Reich for the production of SS uniforms.

Simone feels the pounding in her chest: You're information is correct, monsieur.

Yes, his eyes are arrogant. He gazes at her face and then at her body. He looks down at her shoes and then he looks up at her face again.

You ought to be arrested, Kremer says. How do I know you're not a spy? Isn't it possible you seduce our officers in order to obtain military secrets?

That's absurd, Simone says.

Kremer stares at her: No, madame, it's not absurd. I assure you that it's not absurd. You wouldn't be the first to attempt such a thing. The others are fools, aren't they? I'm not like the others, you know. I'm a member of the SS. Do you know what the SS is?

I'm not a spy.

Kremer waves a hand at her: How do I know that? Maybe you ought to be interrogated by the Gestapo.

Mocking eyes, Simone thinks. She stares at his uniform, at the embroidered bird with spread wings, at the insignia on his collar, at the leather belts across his chest and around his waist. An oberst. Well, it's a higher rank, isn't it? He has a thin face and bony hands. A thin sadistic face. Oh yes, his face is cruel. It's cruel, isn't it? Simone is suddenly aware that she's trembling again.

I think I'd better go, Simone says.

Kremer shakes his head: No, I forbid it.

Simone avoids his eyes: Do you really believe I'm a spy?

It's a possibility, isn't it? In any case, we'll find out sooner or later. One word to the Gestapo and in a few days they'll know everything there is to know about you. Does that frighten you?

Yes, it does frighten me. But I'm not a spy.

Then what are you? Just another French whore from the cafés? Does your husband know? What are you, madame?

Simone's eyes are glazed. She says nothing. She remains motionless as Kremer now steps forward to offer her a cigarette.

Simone is seen from the rear. She stands in the

foreground, almost finished undressing, wearing nothing now but her brassiere and briefs. Her body is visible only from below her shoulders to the middle of her thighs. The shoulder-straps of her brassiere have been pulled down and they dangle on each side, the left shoulder-strap more visible than the right one. Kremer sits in an armchair in the background toward the left. He still wears his uniform. His left hand lies along his thigh near his left knee. He holds a cigarette in his right hand, and now the hand moves and he brings the cigarette to his lips. He puffs at the cigarette once, and then the hand moves again and the cigarette is pulled away. Simone remains motionless. Kremer says nothing. He continues to stare at Simone as he holds the cigarette between two fingers of his right hand.

Now it is Kremer who is closest to the viewer. Only the left part of his body is visible, the left side of his head, his shoulder, his left arm and a small area above the left side of his waist. Simone stands in front of him, bending forward with her arms resting on something, maybe a table or the back of a chair. Her body is turned so that she stands partly with her back toward Kremer and partly in profile. Her brassiere has been removed, and as she bends forward the globe of her right breast is visible between her right forearm and the upper part of her waist. She still wears the briefs. Kremer's right hand is extended, his palm on her right buttock, his fingers splayed out so that his hand covers a wide expanse. For a long moment nothing happens. Then Kremer's right hand appears, the hand moving forward, the fingers finally grasping the top of Simone's briefs around at the front. She turns her head now. Only the upper part of her face is visible as she looks at him over her right shoulder.

The view of Kremer has now changed and he is seen from a forward position and somewhat off to the right side. His right leg is extended in front of him. Simone is naked, standing with her thighs on either side of the leg of Kremer's right boot, leaning forward slightly so that the globes of her breasts dip away from her ribcage.

Kremer's face: the muscles in the face are relaxed, but the eyes show a fixed gaze, either a pensive look or a stare of intense concentration.

Kremer's right boot: the leg of the boot between Simone's thighs now moves upward until it touches the dark thicket of her sex. Simone remains motionless. Kremer continues to raise his leg, the leather of the boot now pressing against her sex.

Simone drops her body a bit, her hips pushing downward, her sex pressing more firmly against the shank of Kremer's right boot. Kremer's face is now seen as he gazes at the junction of his boot and Simone's sex. She continues to push down, her thighs parting as she squats, the lips of her sex visibly opening as they press against the black leather.

Simone looks down. She moves her hips, pushing forward, pulling back, rubbing her sex against the shank of Kremer's right boot. Streaks of wetness are now visible on the black leather. Kremer continues to hold his leg extended. Simone leans forward a bit more and her breasts swing as she moves her body. Her mouth is open, her lips glistening, her face flushed, her head always bent as she continues to look downward.

The movement continues, the open sex rubbing back and forth on Kremer's boot, no sound at all except the faint ticking of a clock somewhere in the shadows.

Simone is kneeling on the floor with the upper part of her body supported by the seat of the sofa. She is seen from her left side, her face turned to the left as she looks over her left arm at the viewer. Only Kremer's boots are visible. He stands behind Simone without moving. Simone now turns her head, her face no longer visible as she looks in the other direction.

Kremer has moved. He now sits on the sofa on the far side of Simone. He sits with his body turned so that he faces the viewer. Simone still has her head turned to the right and her face is hidden. Kremer extends his left hand and he presses his palm against the small of Simone's back. He mumbles something, an indistinct word. Simone opens her thighs wider as Kremer continues to press his left hand against the small of her back near her buttocks.

Now the view has changed and Simone is seen from the rear, her thighs apart, her buttocks and sex exposed. Kremer is still seated beside her on the sofa on her right side. His left hand is still pressing against the small of her back. Now the hand slides over the groove between the two buttocks, the fingers sliding over the anus and down to the bulging sex. He parts the lips of Simone's sex with his fingertips, and then a moment later he slides two fingers inside the mouth of her sex and he pushes them forward until the heel of his palm comes to rest between the globes of her buttocks.

Simone groans.

Kremer slowly pulls his fingers all the way out. The two fingers are visibly wet, the skin glistening between his fingertips and his knuckles. He now touches her anus. He rubs the wet fingertips across the ring of her anus, and then he turns his hand and he wipes the back of his wet fingers across the same spot.

Now the two fingers push forward to enter Simone's

sex again. This time Kremer's thumb comes to rest against the whorl of her anus. His thumb pushes forward, slowly penetrates the dark ring, stretching it as it pushes inside.

Simone groans again: Please . . .

Keep still, Kremer says.

Please, I beg you . . .

He mutters something in German. He pulls his hand back a bit and then he pushes it forward again. Two fingers in her sex and his thumb in her anus. The hand continues to move, the fingers continue to slide.

Simone is now on the sofa, kneeling on the sofa cushion with her head resting on the back of the sofa and both arms extended backward as she holds her buttocks with her hands. She pulls her buttocks apart, exposing the hairy sex, the groove, the dark anus to Kremer's eyes. He stands behind her with his breeches down at his knees and his erect penis in his right hand. He moves closer. He touches the tip of his penis to the ring of Simone's anus. He pushes forward.

Simone groans.

Kremer continues to push forward: Don't move, he says.

Simone remains motionless. She groans again.

Kremer continues to push forward until the entire length of his penis is buried in her bowels. Simone pulls her hands away from her buttocks and she leans her elbows on the back of the sofa. She lifts her head now and she looks back over her right shoulder. Her eyes are glazed, her face flushed, her mouth open.

Kremer is now pulling back. He hesitates. He pushes forward again.

One more week, Kremer says. I leave Paris in a week. It seems they think I'm needed in the east. It's a pity, isn't it? Don't you think it's a pity?

Simone says nothing. She drops her head and she groans as Kremer pushes forward again.

Evening in the Duchenne flat.

Clothilde was here today, Simone says.

Bernard looks at her: Clothilde?

Clothilde Ardry.

What did she want?

It seems Hector has been arrested.

Bernard snorts: I told you it would happen.

Clothilde thought you might help him.

Help him? How can I help him?

Talk to someone, I suppose. He's been arrested by the Gestapo.

That's impossible. I don't know anyone in the Gestapo. And even if I did I wouldn't talk to them. Not about Hector Ardry. Oh no, not about Hector Ardry.

But you've known him such a long time.

That's not true. I hardly know him at all. We never talked to each other at school. I knew nothing about him until he married Clothilde. It was you who introduced us. He's a beggar, isn't he? I'm not talking to the Gestapo about Hector Ardry.

PART THREE: DECEMBER

A stone figure appears on the right, a bent head, an outstretched right arm, part of the figure's chest. The face is seen in profile from the left side, the features molded so that deep shadows appear under the left eye and around the left corner of the mouth. The chin is obscure, more or less obliterated by the shadow. The top of the head is covered with an artifact of some kind, and then it becomes evident the artifact is a sculptured crown of thorns. So the figure is a Christ, and when attention is directed to the extended right arm, the right hand is seen to be pierced by something, no doubt a metal spike or the sculptured equivalent of a metal spike, and in a moment the extension of the crucifix becomes apparent behind the outstretched right arm. And now the shadow cast by the bent head is more prominent, a black profile on the wall under the outstretched right arm, the shadow emphasizing the sharp corners of the crown of thorns, the nose, the entire head of the figure bent in the agony of the crucifixion.

Now at the left, his head almost touching the utmost extension of the crucifix, a priest appears. He stands close to the wall, close enough so that no shadow is visible. He wears black, a white collar displayed at his throat, his head inclined toward his left shoulder, his face impassive, his eyes directed at the stone figure of the crucified Christ.

The priest remains motionless. Nothing moves. Then he turns to his right, turning away from the Christ, and he speaks:

It may be beyond me, the priest says.

Lucien appears. He has been standing out of view to the right of the priest and now he takes a half-step forward as their eyes meet.

Beyond you? Lucien says. What do you mean beyond you?

What you plan to do is a horror.

For them.

Yes, for them, And for everyone.

No, Father, not for everyone. You must remember the cause.

I do remember the cause. I don't like the shedding of blood.

They do their own shedding, don't they?

Dear God.

You must choose, Father.

I'm frightened by the horror.

You need to think of the cause.

I do think of the cause.

*   *   *

Simone is in the metro, seated in a corner of one of the cars of a moving train. The movement of the train, the vibration, the transient jerking of the image is always evident. She sits erect. She holds a purse on her lap, her left hand on the purse and her right hand on the seat beside her. Beyond her left shoulder is one of the windows of the train. A notice has been attached to the window, but the lettering is indistinct and remains uncertain. Apart from the window, the wall of the car is in shadow and obscure. Simone wears a grey cloth coat with a dark fur collar. Two large buttons of the coat are visible between the collar and her waist. She sits with her head lifted a bit, her face without expression, her eyes directed to the right, toward the other passengers. She lowers her head now. She moves the purse in her lap. She places her right hand on top of the purse, her fingers curling around the strap. Then the hand moves again and she slowly unbuttons the top button of the coat she wears. She loosens the fur collar at her throat, and for the first time a blue silk scarf becomes visible. Now she lifts her head again. She glances an instant at the seat beside her, but if the seat is occupied, the occupant is not visible. Only Simone can be seen, Simone alone in the corner of the moving train.

She thinks of uniforms again. Is it that soldier across the aisle? Unterfeldwebel. A sergeant. She knows them all now. How amusing it is. She does have a mind, doesn't she? Schutze oberschutze gefreite obergefreite unteroffizier unterfeldwebel feldwebel oberfeldwebel hauptfeldwebel stabsfeldwebel leutnant oberleutnant hauptmann major oberstleutnant oberst generalmajor generalleutnant general der infanterie generaloberst generalfeldmarschall reichsmarschall. Reichsmarschall Goering has just been meeting with Marshal Pétain in a place called Saint-Florentin-Vergigny in the Occupied Zone. She remembers the photographs in the magazine. She also remembers that Reichsmarschall Goering has a large belly. Not like the officers she knows here in Paris. The Reichsmarschall appears to be immense. Well, it's not the first time she has seen photographs of the Reichsmarschall. In any case, he's in the Luftwaffe and not in the Wermacht. She wonders how Reichsmarschall Goering would look in the black uniform of the SS. She knows them all, too, doesn't she? SS-man sturmmann rottenfuhrer unterscharfuhrer scharfuhrer oberscharfuhrer hauptscharfuhrer untersturmfuhrer obersturmfuhrer hauptsturmfuhrer sturmbannfuhrer obersturmbannfuhrer standartenfuhrer oberfuhrer brigadefuhrer gruppenfuhrer obergruppenfuhrer reichsfuhrer . . .

The train is rocking, the noise of the train rising and falling in synchrony with the sounds of the German military ranks inside Simone's head. She thinks of the uniforms. She thinks of the collar patches, the arm patches, the belts, the tassles, the pistols, the caps, the helmets, the boots. It's madness, darling. It's a complete madness, isn't it? My name is Simone

Duchenne and I'm thirty years old and I think I'm completely mad. It's the rue Lavoisier, isn't it? She spends more and more time in the flat in the rue Lavoisier. She waits for them. She no longer knows their names. Sometimes no one comes to the flat and she waits all afternoon for nothing. Then she lies on the bed naked and she brings herself to orgasm with her fingers. What would Bernard say? Bernard would not believe it. Bernard would say it's beyond belief. But you do it, don't you, darling? You wait for them. The obersts and the oberstleutnants, the uniforms and the boots. My boches. And she gets the pleasure from them one way or the other. They're not all that good at it, you know. Somehow the German military mind does not excel in the arena of the imagination. She knows nothing of the French military mind. God save the French military mind, they didn't do that well, did they? She certainly doesn't want Marie-Claire to marry a French officer. Better a handsome Luftwaffe lieutenant in a white uniform. We are proud to announce the marriage of our daughter Marie-Claire Duchenne to Lieutenant Wilhelm von Schmidt. Yes, why not? They're here to stay, aren't they? Bernard seems to think so. Bernard says they're not fooling us when they talk about a thousand year Reich. Maybe Bernard is thinking of a Duchenne dynasty of uniform manufacturers, Duchenne uniforms for the SS for the next one thousand years. He wants another child. He wants a boy. Two boys. No, I'm finished with that. She had too much trouble with it and she doesn't want it any more. Marie-

Claire is enough. I'm not a cow. He likes to think of
her as a cow, but she's not a cow. My boches don't
think I'm a cow, do they? All that sweating even
when the rooms are cold. They do sweat a great deal,
I don't know why, the Germans do sweat a great
deal, red in the face, the eyes popping, the grunting,
the noises they make, the hands, the twisting fingers,
that stupid bed creaking the way it does, darling, you
want it don't you? Yes you want it, yes you want it,
yes you do want it . . .

Oberst Rademacher is holding a large square of
white paper. He appears to be seated at his desk,
although the desk itself is not visible. He holds the
square of white paper with both hands. Behind him
are the wooden panels of a wall, a vase with red
flowers, a framed photograph on the wall at the left,
a large circular ornament to the right of that, maybe a
souvenir plate or a painted disc of porcelain that
shows two indistinct figures in the midst of what
might be a dance. To the right of the circular ornament, the panelled wall is bare. Oberst Rademacher
sits erect in his chair, the collar of his uniform cutting into the soft flesh under his chin, his mouth
straight, his eyes in shadow so that no expression is
apparent. He moves the white paper in his hands. He
shifts the square of white paper, pushing it forward
and then pulling it back again. Then he rises. He

holds the square of white paper in his hands. He turns to the right and he walks away from the desk.

Now the view has changed and Oberst Rademacher is seen from his right side, standing in profile, the lower part of his body hidden by the back of an upholstered chair, both his hands forward as they hold the square of white paper.

Bernard is in the background. He stands near a large bookcase, his hands folded across the lower part of his belly as he watches Oberst Rademacher. Three sections of the bookcase are visible behind him. High above his head, on one of the molded corners that appear along the top edge of the bookcase, is a figurine, either stone or plaster, a child or an angel, the arrangement of the figure's arms and legs suggesting the figure is in the midst of a dance of some kind.

So this is your plan? Rademacher says.

Bernard nods: Yes.

You're an ambitious man, Monsieur Duchenne. Three thousand uniforms a month. A new factory. I'm impressed.

I want to be of service.

And make a great deal of money.

Yes, I suppose so.

Rademacher laughs: And why not? The Reich doesn't expect you to produce these uniforms for nothing. We're not against business, you know. We're not like the idiot communists, are we?

No.

How many workers do you have now?

Twenty. I'll need one hundred for the new contract.

It's good. I like it. The French people can do more than just send workers to the Reich. There are things to be done here, aren't there? Yes, it's a good idea. I think that's why they approved the small contract so quickly. They like the idea in Berlin. It's a contribution to the war effort, isn't it?

I think of it that way myself.

Do you plan to attend the Christmas Party at the German Institute?

A Christmas party?

Didn't you receive an invitation? I'll have it arranged immediately. You must promise to bring your wife, Monsieur Duchenne. You'll have a chance to meet some important people from Berlin. I hear Himmler may be there. He might have a new idea or two about the uniforms. He's a man with an artistic temperament.

A gray sky. Two o'clock in the afternoon. Bernard is now in the Boulevard des Capucines, euphoric after the meeting with Oberst Rademacher. Three thousand uniforms a month. Himmler at the German Institute. We're making progress, aren't we? And they can't keep the price down forever. If they want quality cloth, they have to pay for it. They're not stupid. They know good cloth is expensive. They know everything.

He wants a cigarette but he realizes he has no

matches. At the next café on the boulevard, he pushes the door forward and he steps inside. He walks to the bar to find the gas to light his cigarette. He's thinking about Rademacher, thinking about Rademacher and Himmler and a million SS uniforms shipped by train in boxes marked Duchenne et Cie. When he finishes lighting the cigarette at the bar, he turns away and the first thing he sees is Nicole sitting against the far wall of the café.

Bernard freezes. He stares at her. She's not alone. She's with a man. Yes, it's the same man, the man he saw on the stairs that day in the rue du Ponceau. Bernard tries to control the shock he feels. It's ridiculous, he thinks. I'm standing here like a clown. He watches them. Nicole is talking. Neither Nicole nor the man are looking in Bernard's direction. Bernard cringes at the possibility that she might see him. Who is the man? He's younger, isn't he? Maybe thirty, maybe younger. Bernard moves behind a pillar. The noise in the café suddenly seems louder. He catches the eyes of the barmaid and he orders a small cognac. Then the smoke from his cigarette gets into his nose and he sneezes. My God, you're a clown, Duchenne. He throws the cognac down his throat and he moves behind the pillar again. The front door flies open and a new crowd pushes its way into the café. Bernard waits another moment, and then he slips through the door without looking at Nicole again.

Lucien. Only his face is visible, part of a hand, a wine glass touching his lips. His hair has been combed back to uncover his forehead. His eyes are directed at the viewer over the edge of the wine glass. Most of his nose is seen through the glass. Behind his head vague shadows are visible, a darker shadow at the lower right, a lighter shadow above that one. The shadows appear to be moving, jerking from side to side then remaining at rest again. Lucien continues to hold the wine glass at his lips. He continues to gaze directly at the viewer.

Now the view changes and more of Lucien can be seen, the people at the tables in the background, the table in front of Lucien. He is no longer with Nicole. A man called Boller is now sitting at the table with Lucien. Boller has a round flat face and horn-rimmed eyeglasses. He appears to be immobilized, his hands folded on the table, his eyes fixed on Lucien as Lucien now pulls the wine glass away from his lips.

What do you think? Lucien says.

Boller continues to stare at him. Then he suddenly shakes himself loose and he shrugs: I don't know. It's dangerous. It's complicated.

Yes, it's complicated.

Listen, we'll have a vote, won't we?

Yes, we'll have a vote.

Give me a cigarette. I need a cigarette.

Lucien pulls out a package of cigarettes and he offers one to Boller.

Are you afraid? Lucien says.

Boller lights the cigarette with his own match before he speaks: I'm not afraid. I don't like it when it's complicated.

*   *   *

Lucien again. He's now outside, alone, walking in
the rue Auber. He wears the black muffler pulled up
to cover his neck and the lower part of his chin. He
stops at the window of a jewelry shop. Wristwatches.
Necklaces. A fake gold bracelet. He turns away and
he begins walking again. Scraps of paper blow at his
feet. In a moment two German soldiers pass him, one
of the soldiers laughing at something. They ignore
Lucien. He continues on his path. Now a woman, a
pedestrian on the pavement, a well-dressed woman
wearing a dark coat with a fur collar walks toward
him. Their eyes meet. Lucien does not know her.
The woman turns her eyes away. They pass each
other. The woman is Simone Duchenne. Lucien continues walking.

Simone entering the jewelry shop in the rue Auber.
She has the fur collar of her coat turned up to cover
the back of her neck. She wears a tight-fitting hat
pulled down on the right side to almost cover her
right eye. Her lips are painted dark red, the lower lip
glistening now in the light from one of the overhead
lamps. Behind her is a dark square, maybe a window
or one of the display cases in the shop, to the right of
that an arrangement of dark vertical lines that might
be the edge of another cabinet.

As she approaches one of the counters, a clerk

arrives on the other side. The clerk is a thin man with a moustache. He wears a dark suit, a tie, a white handkerchief in his left breast pocket. He smiles. He speaks to Simone. She answers him. The words are indistinct. Her lips move, but the words are ambiguous. The clerk nods and he walks away. Simone stands there with her eyes on the glass of the counter, the arrangement of bracelets in a series of trays lined with black velvet. Before long the clerk returns. He carries a small package and a slip of paper. Simone signs the slip of paper. She removes some paper money from her purse and she hands it to the clerk. He smiles as he hands the package to her. Simone places the package inside her purse and she turns away from the counter to leave the shop.

She won't like them, Simone thinks. Simone is in the street now. Marie-Claire won't like them. Simone has just bought Marie-Claire three of those Pétain medallions. One hundred twenty francs. It's an absurdity. The girl is a child and she knows nothing about Pétain. She calls Pétain the old man with the white moustache. She knows nothing. It's madness. Yes, you're going mad, Simone thinks. This is how it starts, isn't it? Stupid little impulses that make no sense. She has bouts of anxiety these days, her pulse racing, her breath short. The other day in a department store she thought she might faint. And when she finds herself alone it's one compulsion after the other. Count the words in a magazine she's reading. Count the lines on a page. When she crosses the carpet in the sitting room, she feels compelled to step on certain parts of the pattern. In the street she always makes certain to avoid any cracks in the pavement. It's the beginning of madness, isn't it? Yes, she knows it. You'll be mad, darling. They'll shake their heads when they talk about you. In the evening she locks herself in the bathroom and an hour passes as she carefully examines every centimeter of her body. Is this a bruise? Did she get that today? And here. What's this? Who was it that bit her nipple the other day? Bernard sees nothing. Bernard hardly looks at her when she's naked. Not that she minds. She doesn't care. She doesn't care whether Bernard looks at her or whether he doesn't look at her or what he thinks. You're trembling, darling. Yes, you're trembling. You're trembling, aren't you?

Simone is now at the entrance of a cinema. She hesitates. She looks at the posters announcing the film. MARIE STUART. With Zarah Leander and Willy Birgel. She finally enters the lobby and she buys a ticket.

The usher, a woman dressed in black with a white apron, leads Simone to a seat in the dark theater. Simone tips the woman and she sits down. Well, this is not Marie Stuart, is it? These are soldiers at war somewhere. A narrator speaks: FOLLOWING THE SOVIET TROOPS IN RETREAT, THE GERMAN ARMY ENTERS A BURNING VILLAGE. The camera is behind the German soldiers. The burning village is on the right side of the road. Two dozen German soldiers are visible, two artillery pieces on wheels being pushed and dragged by the soldiers, the village burning, the smoke rising in clouds of black and white and gray.

Then another scene. The narrator speaks again: PRECEDING THE INFANTRY, MOTORCYCLISTS ARE HOLDING A STRATEGIC BRIDGE AFTER SEVERAL HOURS OF COMBAT. Two motorcyclists are visible on the bridge. The dirt road is in the foreground. In the background, the horizon is obscured by black and gray smoke. The silhouette of a burning truck appears on the right.

And then a scene like the first, this time the camera much closer to the advancing soldiers. ANOTHER INFANTRY GROUP MOVING THROUGH A STREET BORDERED BY HOUSES IN FLAMES. Is that snow on the road? The flames of the burning house on the right appear about to burst into the theater. Simone closes her eyes. The narrator continues talking. Simone keep her eyes closed. The words of the narrator become incomprehensible. Simone keeps her eyes closed.

In the flat in the rue du Ponceau, Bernard is seated on the sofa with Nicole on his lap. Both Bernard and

Nicole are seen from their right sides. Bernard is
stripped to the waist. Nicole still wears her dress, but
the shoulders and the front of the dress have been
pulled down and she now has her arms folded across
the top of the dress to hold it in place over her
breasts. Bernard's right arm is around Nicole's waist.
Nicole's head is turned as she looks over her right
shoulder at Bernard's face. Her mouth is open, her
lower teeth visible. Behind Nicole, a small lamp is
visible in a corner of the room.

Where will you be on Christmas Day? Nicole says.

Bernard shrugs: I don't know. With my family, I
suppose.

Well, I'll be alone.

No family?

There's only my brother. I don't know if we'll be
together.

Why not?

I don't know.

Pull your dress down in front.

But why? It's too cold in here.

It's not cold. I like it when your breasts are free.

Nicole makes a sound with her lips: You're a pig,
aren't you?

Bernard and Nicole are naked on the bed, Nicole
on all fours and Bernard behind her with his penis
slowly thrusting in and out of her sex. They are both
seen from their right sides. Nicole has her head down

as she supports the front part of her body with her hands on the pillow. Bernard has his hands between Nicole's hips and her ribcage, although only his right hand is completely visible. The bedsheet and the blanket have been pushed down to the foot of the bed. In the background is the wall, the pattern of the wallpaper definite and sharp, a painting on the left side, a smaller painting on the right side, an ornament of some kind attached to the wall between the two paintings. The painting on the left side shows a muddy landscape. The painting on the right side is ambiguous, a suggestion of an arrangement of flowers, blues and greens and yellows. Bernard pulls back, the shaft of his penis shining, then he pushes forward again. His scrotum appears swollen, the dark hair covering the sac only incompletely hiding the wrinkled skin. His head is bent as he looks down at his moving organ. Now the pace quickens. He pushes forward, pulls back, pushes forward again. His hands grasp more firmly at Nicole's waist. She keeps her head down, the lower part of her face hidden by her right arm, her body immobilized as the penis continues moving in and out of her sex. Bernard makes a sound. He shudders. He makes another sound. He pushes forward and he lifts his head, his eyes closed and his mouth open, his pelvis grinding against Nicole's buttocks.

I saw you with a man, Bernard says.

Nicole is lying on the bed while Bernard gets dressed. She looks at him: A man?

In the Boulevard des Capucines. In a café.

Nicole shrugs: My brother.

Should I believe that?

He's my brother.

What's his name?

Lucien.

I don't believe you.

But it's true. You don't have any reason to be jealous. It was only my brother. It's amusing.

Bernard slides his tie under the collar of his shirt: It's not amusing.

It's amusing that you're jealous of my brother.

Does he come here?

Yes, he comes here. He likes to visit me.

What does he do? Does he have a job?

Nicole hesitates, her eyes turning away: It's better not to talk about it.

What do you mean?

I said I don't want to talk about it.

I want to know.

He works for the resistance.

Bernard's face: he stares at his own face in the mirror. His hands continue working at his tie, tightening the knot, adjusting the knot at the collar of his shirt. Then he turns and he faces Nicole again. The blanket has been pulled up to cover the upper half of her body, but her legs and most of thighs are exposed.

Are you telling me the truth? Bernard says.

Nicole shrugs: Of course.

He's a fool.

I don't know. Sometimes I work for them, too.

You're lying.

No, it's true. I follow people. They tell me who to follow and I follow them.

What for?

I don't know. To see where they go, I suppose.

Bernard stares at her legs, at her painted toenails. For a long moment he remains motionless, standing beside the bed with his eyes on Nicole's legs. Then Nicole shifts her body on the bed. She sits up with her back against the headboard and her breasts covered by the blanket.

What's the matter? Nicole says.

Bernard appears to twist his neck to the side. He sits down on the edge of the bed and he pulls at the blanket to uncover Nicole's breasts. He takes her right breast in his left hand. He slides his thumb over the nipple.

Did you spend all the money I gave you?

I still have a few hundred francs.

He pulls at her nipple with his fingertips: You're a lucky girl to have nipples like these.

In the sitting room in the flat in the rue Lavoisier, Simone is with a colonel named Beckmann, once a lawyer in Frankfurt and now a Wermacht oberst in Paris. They each hold a wine glass, Beckmann's glass in his left hand, Simone's glass in her right hand.

Beckmann's neatly pressed uniform appears more grey than green in the dim artificial light that comes from somewhere on the left. Beckmann and Simone stand at one of the walls in the sitting room, Beckmann on the right, his right shoulder leaning against the wall, his head inclined toward his left shoulder as he gazes at Simone who stands close to him on the left. Simone appears to be leaning her back against the wall, her face turned away from Beckmann toward her right shoulder and the glass of wine she holds in her right hand. She wears nothing above the waist except a necklace with an attached pendant that almost reaches the valley between her breasts. The pale blue skirt shows a series of folds and ruffles and bows just below the waist, but it's not clear whether the top of the dress has been pulled down or whether the dress is no more than a skirt made to be worn with a blouse. The skirt reaches a few inches below Simone's knees. She wears dark stockings, but the lower parts of her legs and her shoes are obscured by deep shadows. The edge of a small table appears on Simone's right side, the corner of the table apparently touched by the lower part of her right hip. The wall behind Beckmann's head shows a small framed watercolor behind glass, a landscape or a bed of flowers in reds and yellows and blues.

Beckmann lifts his wine glass. He sips the wine. He gazes at Simone's breasts again.

Simone is now naked. Oberst Beckmann wears

only his dark grey socks. He lies on his back on the bed as Simone straddles his body on all fours. Beckmann's head rests on a large white pillow. The tip of Beckmann's penis can be seen penetrating Simone's sex, but the shaft of the penis glistens with Simone's secretions, suggesting the penis has already made several complete entries. Simone's hands are on the bed, her arms supporting the weight of the front·part of her body, her face lifted, her breasts dangling over Beckmann's face. Most of Beckmann's face is hidden by Simone's left breast, only the right side of his forehead and part of his right eye visible at the edge of Simone's left forearm. It is not clear whether or not Beckmann is sucking her left breast. Beckmann's arms encircle Simone's waist just above the curve of her buttocks. She straddles Beckmann's body with her knees wide apart, her sex (now pene-trated by the tip of Beckmann's penis) and anus fully exposed to the viewer. Beckmann's knees are also wide apart, the entire shaft of his penis and his pink scrotum fully revealed. Only the left side of Simone's face is visible. Her eyes appear to be closed, her mouth open just enough to show a space between her lips.

Simone moves. She lowers her hips, the mouth of her sex slowly engulfing the rigid penis. She contin-ues to push down until only the very base of the penis is still visible, the base of the penis and the bulging scrotum below it. After a moment of hesita-tion, Simone moves again, her hips moving upward,

Beckmann's penis gradually reappearing, the entire length of the penis once again exposed until only the tip remains inside the mouth of Simone's sex. Beckmann's hands now leave Simone's waist to slide over the globes of her buttocks. He holds her buttocks as she pushes downward again. His fingers can be seen squeezing into the smooth flesh, his hands grasping at the two globes. The movement is continuous now, Simone's hips lifting and dropping and then lifting again, Beckmann's hands grasping her buttocks, Simone's eyes remaining closed, her mouth open, her face tilted upward, her hips moving up and then down again . . .

Bernard is in the metro, on the platform of the Reaumur-Sebastopol station. He stands in the foreground, behind three helmeted German soldiers. He wears a grey fedora hat and a dark coat. He stands with his hands in the pockets of his coat and his eyes on the shaved neck of one of the soldiers.

It must be heavy on the head, Bernard thinks. The German helmets must be heavy on the head. More substantial than the French helmets. Bernard remembers the helmet he wore in 1916. Heavy on head, wasn't it? And this is more substantial. He's thankful he's not a soldier. Where is the train? You're afraid, aren't you? Yes, he's afraid. How stupid she is. That stupid little bitch in the resistance. And her brother.

Is he really her brother? If she gets arrested, what then? They question her, don't they? Mademoiselle Sabatier, please tell us who pays the rent for your flat. And of course she tells them it's a man called Bernard Duchenne, he owns a factory but I don't know much about him. And the Fritz smiles at her: Well, mademoiselle, you may know more than you think. Then after the smile he slaps her face. Once on each side. Then he pulls the front of her dress down to get her breasts out. He plays with her breasts awhile and then finally the interrogation specialist arrives and he takes over. Does he wear a white coat? Yes, maybe he wears a white coat. He's a specialist, isn't he? He works on her breasts first. On her nipples. She screams and she cries. Tell us everything you know about Monsieur Duchenne, he says. Is he in the resistance? She says no and he works on her nipples again. He continues working on her nipples until she says yes, Monsieur Duchenne is in the resistance. And who else? She tells them her brother is also in the resistance. Do they know each other? I don't think so. Another twist of the left nipple and she says yes, I think they know each other. And so on and so on. Are you afraid, Bernard? Yes, I'm afraid. Rademacher won't help, will he? What does the specialist do when the subject is male and not female? No pretty breasts available for the interrogation. Then it's the balls, isn't it? The specialist shrugs and he works on the balls.

When the train finally arrives, Bernard follows the

three German soldiers and he hears them laughing as both soldiers and civilians push their way into the crowded car.

Lucien and Nicole are seated at the wooden table in the kitchen of the flat in the rue du Ponceau. Two empty chairs are visible in the foreground. On the other side of the table, behind Lucien and Nicole, stands a long buffet on top of which is arrayed a line of jars and dishes. Lucien wears a blanket around his shoulders and he has his head turned as he looks over his left shoulder at Nicole. She wears a blouse and a skirt, but only part of the skirt is visible under the edge of the table in front of her. She sits near Lucien with the upper part of her body turned away from him, her left elbow resting on the back of the wooden chair, her left hand supporting the side of her head, her right forearm on the edge of the table, the fingers of her right hand curled around a tall glass.

Lucien says nothing. He turns his head to his right and he stares straight ahead for a long moment. Then he turns his head back and once again he gazes at Nicole.

Why don't you believe me? Lucien says.

Nicole sighs. She turns the upper part of her body and she faces Lucien: I don't care.

After the explosion they'll arrest hundreds. And some of my friends, too. Maybe someone will talk.

They'll tell them about me. They'll tell them I have a sister.

Will they arrest Blanche?

She's leaving Paris. She'll be across the line before it happens.

Will they arrest the sisters of all your friends?

I want you to leave Paris.

I don't have any money. How can I leave if I don't have any money?

I'll get you the money. I'll get you the money and a pass in a few days.

Nicole sighs again: I don't care.

Lucien groans: I want you to leave Paris.

Bernard is in his office, the line of workers at their sewing machines visible through the glass windows. He sits at his desk with his eyes on the clock. The pendulum of the clock swings back and forth. Bernard stares at the hands of the clock as he thinks of Nicole again. Maybe it's a lie, he thinks. Maybe what she told him is a lie. Maybe she has no brother. No one in the resistance and not her in the resistance. Why would they have her in the resistance? She can't do anything. What would they want with a girl like Nicole? It's absurd. She can't be in the resistance. And if she's not in the resistance, then she doesn't have a brother. What she has is a lover. No, you're a fool, what she has is a brother and the brother is in the resistance. And Nicole, too. And that means sooner or later the Gestapo will arrest Bernard Duchenne. The Gestapo will hold Bernard Duchenne as a hostage and sooner or later Bernard Duchenne will be shot. They don't care about the contract for uniforms. Rademacher will find someone else. In the meantime I'll be dead and buried and not thinking about uniforms any more. I don't want to die, Bernard thinks. He's on the edge of something big, isn't he? He could make a pile in the next year or two. This is not the time for difficulties. The boches are here and this is not the time for any difficulties. You're afraid, aren't you? Yes, I'm afraid. I don't want any difficulties. What man in his right mind would want any difficulties at a time like this? I have a child. I have a daughter named Marie-Claire. I have a wife. Does it make any difference if you tell them that? It doesn't make any difference at all. I have a contract with the Reich to produce uniforms for the SS. I demand to see some official from the SS. Are you a saboteur, Monsieur Duchenne? Any friends in the resistance? I don't care about the resistance. Then what is it you care about? I care about the New Order. Ha ha. That's it. I care about the New Order. I intend to enroll at Berlitz next week to improve my knowledge of German. My present energies are directed toward the production of first class uniforms for the SS. Yes, of course, the Reich pays a high price for these uniforms, but you must remember that expenses in Paris these days are terrible. Do I pay the rent for the flat occupied by Nicole Sabatier? Yes, I pay for that flat in the rue du Ponceau. I admit to a weakness for young women of a certain type. Surely as a man you can understand that? Even in the New Order there must be room for certain emotional necessities. Ha ha. We understand each other, don't we? But this one is not the specialist. When the specialist arrives, they won't let me talk so much. The idea is to have them declare you innocent before the specialist arrives. And all because of that little bitch Nicole. You're a fool, Duchenne. You're a fool, aren't you? No, I'm not a fool, I'm not a fool. When a problem exists, you find the solution, eh?

The pendulum of the clock continues to swing back and forth, back and forth. Bernard stares at the hands of the clock. His eyes see nothing. He sits immobilized at his desk, his hands folded in front of him, his eyes on the clock, on the pendulum, on the hands of the clock.

Then finally his body jerks and he looks alert again. He opens a drawer on the right side of the desk and he pulls out a small card. He closes the door and he places the card directly in front of him. Then he reaches for the telephone. He lifts the receiver and he begins dialing: TURbigo 92-00.

The connection is made. Thin squawking sounds on the other end of the line. Bernard hesitates a moment, and then he turns his back to the glass wall of the office and he speaks into the mouthpiece of the telephone:

Duchenne here, D-U-C-H-E-N-N-E, Bernard Duchenne. I'm calling to provide the police with information about two people . . .

Bernard's voice gradually fades, the sound replaced by the noise of the sewing machines outside the office, the view changing, the line of women appearing, their fingers pushing at black cloth under the moving needles.

And now the small factory is empty except for Bernard and the seamstress Eva. She sits in his office on the wooden chair near the door. Bernard stands leaning against the edge of his desk with his arms folded. They look at each other. No one moves. Nothing is heard except the ticking of the large clock on the wall near Bernard's desk. Eva sits with her hands in her lap. Bernard now unfolds his arms and he puts his hands in his pockets. He continues looking at her, his eyes on her face, on the curves of her breasts revealed by the tight red sweater. Her skirt covers her knees. She wears brown stockings and brown shoes. She sits with her knees together and her feet flat on the floor. Now she moves her legs. She crosses her right knee over her left knee and she pulls at the hem of her skirt to cover her knees again. Bernard gazes at her legs a moment longer and then he lifts his eyes to her face. The ticking of the clock is still the only sound in the small room.

Bernard looks at her red lips. He wonders about her family. Does she have a family? Yes, she has a husband and a young son. She told him she has a husband and a young son. The husband delivers bread.

Or is it cheese? Bernard does not remember. He
thinks about her buttocks. A woman like this one
ought to have a firm bottom. Like Nicole. Eva is
much older than Nicole and broader in the hips, but
Bernard suspects that Eva has a firm bottom. In any
case, he does not want to think about Nicole now.
The business with Nicole is finished, isn't it? He
thinks about Eva. She has a fine mouth, the lips full
and soft-looking and painted a bright red. Bernard
feels a thrill of anticipation as he gazes at Eva's
bright red mouth. He looks at the clock. He looks at
the telephone on his desk and then he looks away
because he does not want to think about Nicole again.
Instead he looks at Eva again:

There's that little hotel down the street, Bernard
says. Why don't we try that one?

Two straining bodies in a small room with grimy
curtains. Eva lies on her back with Bernard between
her thighs. The light of the lamp falls on the bed and
the two bodies are clearly revealed. Bernard supports
the upper part of his body with his arms, his hips
pumping, his penis sliding in and out of Eva's gaping
sex. She's much hairier than he expected, dark hair
on the lower part of her belly and the insides of her
thighs and in the groove between her buttocks. The
sex itself is loose and full and quite different than
Nicole's. He was right about Eva's buttocks. She has
a hard bottom. She moves her hips now. She lifts her

knees and she opens her thighs wide. Bernard continues thrusting in her sex, and then he suddenly pulls himself out of her. Eva makes a sound in her throat as she stares at him.

Turn over, Bernard says. Get on your knees.

She hesitates a moment, her eyes fixed on his face. Then she does what he wants. She rolls over on the bed and she lifts the lower part of her body so that now she's on all fours with her rear pointing at Bernard. Is it bread or cheese? Bernard thinks. He can't remember what it is that her husband delivers to the restaurants in St. Germain. He gazes down at the dark split between the two buttocks. He palms each globe. He rubs the ball of his right thumb over the crinkled rose of her anus. The sphincter tightens and then relaxes again. Bernard gathers saliva in his mouth and in a moment his spits the saliva directly into the groove. That's much better. Now he rubs her anus with his thumb again. Eva mumbles something as his thumb slips inside. She has her head and shoulders down on the mattress now and Bernard is aware of nothing except the lower part of her body, the broad rump, the full thighs, the strong legs. She mumbles again when he pushes the knob of his penis inside her anus. Then a groan. Eva groans as he pushes forward.

It's good, Bernard thinks. She's as good as Nicole. He won't have her in the rue du Ponceau because it's too elegant for her. But it's good anyway. Yes, it's quite good, isn't it? It's quite good.

* * *

Good evening, madame.

Simone nods to the young boy on the stairs as she enters the Duchenne flat. Marie-Claire comes running out of one of the rooms with a large doll in her hands.

Mommy, I have a new doll.

A new doll? Where did you get it?

Aunt Hélène sent it to me.

How lovely, darling. She's a pretty little girl, isn't she?

Now Simone is alone in the sitting room. She's had a difficult afternoon and she's exhausted. Another colonel, this one from Munich. A robust animal. Oh yes, what an animal he was. Simone quivers as she thinks of it. All that sweat on his body. How many now, darling? All that boche sperm inside and outside her body. Do an accounting, will you? Count all the names. Well, I can't, I don't remember all the names. Then I'll count the faces. Do I remember all the faces? No, I don't remember all the faces either. I remember nothing. I remember everything. How many years have passed since the first of them? I'm an old woman. All that sperm. It ages the face, doesn't it? Madame Simone Duchenne naked in the arms of the German conquerors. It's madness, isn't it? I'm trembling. I have the smell of sweat and sex in my nose. This one today amused himself by ejaculating on her breasts. She didn't mind it. She liked it. When she was alone in the bathroom, she smeared the sperm over her nipples. All that fresh sperm glistening on her breasts. Quiring did that once. Where is Quiring now? Is he in Russia? In the midst of winter on the eastern front? They'll have Russia, too, won't they? Bernard says they'll have everything. And you, darling? What will you have? I'll have my boches, won't I?

Late evening in the sitting room. Bernard reads his newspapers. *La Gerbe* now. Simone is once again looking at the Christmas issue of *L'Illustration*. The price is 40 francs. Four sculptured figures on the cover, a painted bas-relief from somewhere. A young woman and a child on the left, a young man in the center, another young woman on the right, this one with her breasts exposed. Eleventh or twelfth century, Simone thinks. The breasts of the young woman on the right are like firm little apples.

Did you have a nice day? Bernard says.

Simone looks at him: Yes, of course. And you?

Good. Quite good. I'm optimistic about the future.

The future?

I mean the political situation. The occupation. I think Hitler means to have us as an equal partner soon. We'll be part of it, won't we?

I don't know.

Yes, I think so. You look distracted. Is anything wrong?

No, I'm fine.

You do look distracted.

But I'm fine.

What did you do today? I thought the weather was pleasant.

I went shopping. I bought a few things for Marie-Claire.

Is the new maid satisfactory?

Yes, I think so.

She'll have to last the winter, won't she? It's always difficult to get them in the winter months.

I think this one will stay.

Bernard nods: I'm expecting to hear from Berlin soon. Important people.

More uniforms?

Yes. Everything is going quite well.

Well, I'm glad.

I have a surprise.

A surprise.

Yes, but you must wait. I need some time to prepare it. Five minutes or so.

Simone is puzzled. She watches Bernard as he leaves the sitting room. She wonders what the surprise is. She opens the magazine again, her fingers turning the pages, one colored picture after the other. Reproductions of the paintings of Claude Monet. An illustrated article about Anna Iaroslawna, Queen of France in the eleventh century. A collection of painted ceramic figurines. Another collection of paintings: childhood as seen by the painter Berthe Morisot. The Sleeping Naiad, an under-the-sea story by Pierre Valmigere, illustrated by Jean A. Mercier. An illus-

trated article on the new decorations of the cathedral
of Vich. And near the end of the magazine a display
of furs in high fashion: Paquin, A. Leroy, Nina
Ricci, Weil. Simone studies the furs, the models in
the furs. She likes the coat by Nina Ricci. Something
unusual. The collar is high and flares out like the
wings of a bat. Well, it's chic, isn't it? Yes, she
does like it.

Bernard's voice: What do you think?

Simone looks up and she feels an abrupt shock, a
dislocation, her mind reeling. Bernard is wearing a
black uniform. All black. Cap and tunic and breeches
and boots. It's the SS. Oh, she knows it, doesn't she?

I had it made for me, Bernard says. Don't you like
it?

He puts his hands on his hips and he moves his
legs apart. He stands facing her. Simone reads the
collar insignia. He's a colonel, isn't he? An Oberst in
the SS. The cap has the death's head emblem on the
front of the crown. The white piping is elegant. The
boots have a high polish. He's not Bernard. No, this
is really Bernard, isn't it? I don't know. She rises.
She goes to him. Bernard takes her in his arms. He
makes her turn. He presses her against the wall. He
bends his head and he kisses her mouth.

Sunday afternoon. This is the 21st of December in
the year 1941. They like to walk in the park on
Sundays, in the Tuileries and around the Place du

Carrousel. They walk hand-in-hand, Bernard and Marie-Claire and Simone, Bernard on the left and Marie-Claire in the middle and Simone on the right. The sun is shining today. The air is crisp and cool four days before Christmas. The sparrows flutter from one barren tree to the next. Marie-Claire says something and Bernard laughs. Marie-Claire swings her arms, swinging the arms of her parents. They walk west in the Tuileries, and viewed from behind the Duchennes appear silhouetted against a bright sky. From a distance one can still recognize them: a man and a woman with a child between them, three figures walking slowly in an empty park.

☾ BLUE MOON BOOKS

____ EVELINE/65001/$3.95
____ "FRANK" AND I/65002/$3.95
____ A MAN WITH A MAID/65003/$3.95
____ ROMANCE OF LUST BOOK I/65004/$3.95
____ SECRET TALENTS/65005/$3.95
____ THE BOUDOIR/65006/$3.95
____ DREAM BOAT/65007/$3.95
____ PLEASURE BOUND/65008/$3.95
____ LA VIE PARISIENNE/65009/$3.95
____ VENUS SCHOOL MISTRESS/65010/$3.95
____ SWEET DREAMS/65011/$3.95
____ SUBURBAN SOULS BOOK I/65012/$3.95
____ LOVE LESSONS/65013/$3.95
____ ROMANCE OF LUST BOOK II/65014/$3.95
____ WOMAN OF THE MOUNTAIN, WARRIORS
       OF THE TOWN/65015/$3.95
____ SUBURBAN SOULS BOOK II/65016/$3.95
____ THE OXFORD GIRL/65017/$4.50
____ BLUE TANGO/65018/$4.50
____ GREEN GIRLS/65019/$3.95
____ MISS HIGH HEELS/65020/$3.95
____ RUSSIAN ROULETTE: THE SOVIET
       ADVENTURES OF PROFESSOR
       SPENDER/65021/$4.50
____ IRONWOOD/65022/$4.50
____ THOMASINA/65023/$4.50
____ THE CALAMITIES OF JANE/65024/$3.95
____ AN ENGLISH EDUCATION/65025/$4.50
____ THE RITES OF SODOM: PROFESSOR SPENDER'S
       MIDDLE EASTERN TRIP/65026/$4.50
____ MY SECRET LIFE/65027/$7.95
____ DREAMS OF FAIR WOMEN/65028/$4.50
____ SABINE/65029/$4.50
____ THE TUTOR'S BRIDE/65030/$4.50
____ A WEEKEND VISIT/65031/$4.50
____ THE RECKONING/65032/$4.50
____ THE INTERRUPTED BOSTON/65033/$4.50
____ CAROUSEL/65034/$4.50